The Politician's Heart

Michel Prince

The Growing Strong Series
Book 3

LGBT Romance

S

Published by
Satin Romance
An Imprint of Melange Books, LLC
White Bear Lake, MN 55110
www.satinromance.com

ISBN: 978-1-68046-389-7

Cover Design by Ashley Byland from Redbird Designs

The girls of Growing Strong have become best friends to us all and I thank my readers for coming back to see what's happening next in their lives.

My family for their support. My editor for never letting me get an inch and Satin Romance for letting me keep the girls out there.

Chapter One

"Someday you're gonna look back on this moment of your life as such a sweet time of grieving. You'll see that you were in mourning and your heart was broken, but your life was changing..."
—Elizabeth Gilbert

February

Sarah Lindstrom's hands glided down her girlfriend's bare arms. Sarah loved the feel of Lisa's smooth satin skin after she toweled off and lotioned herself. Her short, black hair was still damp and smelled of lilacs bringing spring into her dark winter's night.

Kneeling on the bed, Sarah rested her head on Lisa's shoulder.

"All right, what is it?" Lisa teased as her hand reached back to cradle Sarah's head and keep her close.

"What do you mean?"

"You've been extremely snuggly the last few days, and I doubt it's because of Valentine's Day."

Lisa turned her head to the side so her pale, green eyes would make Sarah speak the truth. Something about her eyes could unlock every secret Sarah held close to her heart. That's how Sarah knew Lisa was the one she couldn't live without, and even though she had it all planned out for Valentine's Day, Sarah smiled and finally asked.

"Marry me?" The butterflies were at warp speed in her belly even if her head couldn't have been clearer.

"You're funny," Lisa said as she got up off the bed and crossed to the dresser, ripping the air from Sarah's lungs as she did.

"It's legal now, you know?"

"Yes, I'm very aware of that." Lisa pulled a sweatshirt out of her drawer and covered the little bit of exposed skin left from her camisole.

Sarah could feel the cold wall Lisa put up sometimes when she'd come to a place she didn't want to venture.

"Lisa, you do want to be with me, right?"

Lisa turned and gave the condescending face Sarah had gotten used to over the last few years. It was supposed to be her '*awe baby, you know I love you face*', but Sarah knew better. It was more of an '*if I have sex with you, can this conversation be over*'? face.

"Baby, you know—"

Sarah held up her hand to cut Lisa off. "Why did you insist on going to the capital to protest day after day?"

Lisa rocked back on her heels, and then headed toward the living room. Sarah leapt from the bed and stopped her at the bedroom door.

"Where are you going?"

"I need to take a drive."

"You need to stay and talk this out."

"Talk what out? Geez Sarah, you're so dramatic over every little thing."

"Dramatic? I just asked you to marry me."

"I don't think you fully understand what that means, honey."

If there was one thing Sarah hated more than the 'awe baby' face, it was when Lisa acted as if Sarah were still a child. She was twenty-five to Lisa's thirty-two, but that didn't change the fact that Sarah was leaps and bounds more mature than Lisa would ever be.

"Enlighten me, o-ancient-one."

"Childish," she chided back.

"We love each other. I know I want to spend the rest of my life with you."

"Awe, baby," Lisa said as she cradled Sarah's face in her hands. "I love you, too."

Awe baby…that told Sarah more than anything ever could. Lisa 'awe, babied' half the people she worked with at the spa right before she dumped a crap load of work on them. "Awe, baby," she'd start, "you're so good at that, could you unload the truck that just brought three new massage tables? Awe baby, if you aren't the sweetest thing ever, could you do the laundry for me?"

"I thought we were building a life together. Isn't that why you moved in with me?" Sarah held in the tears that burned in her eyes.

"Awe—" Sarah's hand shot up so fast to silence Lisa she almost backhanded her. Lisa's sing song voice dissipated as she finally spoke truthfully to Sarah. "What do you want from me, Sarah? Get married, buy a starter home, and adopt a couple of kids from China or Guatemala? Better yet, how about we both get inseminated on the same day until one of us gets pregnant?" Lisa clapped her hands together in feigned excitement. "Maybe we'll both get pregnant at the same time and we can have twins, because of course we'd use the same donor."

"You're not funny," Sarah said as she turned and crossed to the window. Looking out to the snow covered parking lot of their apartment as an orange light flashed from the plow, her head felt thick and heavy as thoughts screamed at her. How had it all fallen apart? Had she missed the signs?

"I'm realistic," Lisa sighed. "You're not."

"What's so bad about having a real home together? Even a kid or two? Isn't that why we fought to have the right to marry? The right for you to be in the room if, God forbid, I get some terminal disease."

"I wouldn't be the one in the room and we both know it."

Sarah turned to look at her.

"Why not? I'd be there in a heartbeat if I ever heard you were sick or injured."

"Mary Beth would be there, Gabbie or Mandy, they've always come before me, and even if they didn't, I'm not the type of person that's there to hold your hand in the end. I'm the person that'll put you in the hospital."

"You're jealous of my friends? I've put you before them on so many occasions I'm surprised they still talk to me some days."

"Look, Sarah, it's been fun, but obviously, we've come to the end."

"I ask you to marry me and you break up with me? You can throw away two great years that easily?"

"I could tell you were getting more clingy. It seemed as if you wanted more. I wasn't really surprised when you asked me."

"You already have someone new, don't you?"

"Don't be paranoid." Lisa pushed past Sarah and snagged her keys from the kitchen counter.

"I'm dramatic and paranoid." Sarah held her hand to her chest, and then dropped it quickly. "I guess I'm also an idiot, because I believed you loved me."

"Your friends are all pairing up and you're just playing at being a lesbian. You want a picket fence and two point three kids like every hetero you know."

"I want a family with the woman I love. That's not gay or straight, that's human."

"Keep telling yourself that," Lisa mocked. "I've tried to bring you into the lifestyle, but you insist on hanging on to your past."

"You love the sound of your voice, don't you? It doesn't matter if what you say even makes sense."

"Why would you even want to get married?"

"Five minutes ago I could have answered you instantly." Sarah ran her hand over her hair. "Now, I guess I should be thanking you for saying no."

"Yes, you should." Lisa raised her eyebrow.

"How about I leave," Sarah said, reaching for her jacket and keys. "You pack."

After driving aimlessly for an hour, Sarah turned into the apartment building of one of her best friends, Mary Beth Wallace.

Mary Beth had been in trouble seven years ago and gotten pregnant. The two of them, along with their friends Mandy and Gabbie, used their college funds to buy a business—Growing Strong Montessori Day Care Center. After enrolling in classes to be certified caregivers for young children, first the simple early childhood educators, then the Montessori training center, the three of them went from taking over a day care center to creating a school. They had recently acquired an abandoned St. Paul School District building and were bringing the old school back to life.

With her messenger bag still in the car, she had an excuse to see Mary Beth. Since it was almost ten, Sarah knocked lightly to not wake up Mary Beth's six year old, Luke.

Sarah drifted, trying to find an anchor to hold on to. Maybe Lisa was right, she did depend on her friends too much, but when Mary Beth opened the door Sarah instantly felt warmth creep into her bones.

"Sarah? What's up?" Mary Beth asked as she smoothed back her short, red hair. Mary Beth's hazel eyes, with green speckles, looked worried at her friend's sudden, late night arrival.

"I thought you'd want to work on our presentation for a few hours tonight."

"At ten o'clock?"

"Is it that late already?"

"Come in," Mary Beth said as she opened her door wider and Sarah caught sight of Eli, Mary Beth's boyfriend, on the couch. When he saw Sarah he stood up and headed for the door.

"I don't want to disturb you."

"It's okay," Eli said with his hands up in surrender. "I know better than to mess with the mafia."

Eli gave Mary Beth a quick kiss, then whispered a few words in her ear before he left.

"I really didn't—" Sarah began, and Mary Beth held up her hand to stop her as she opened the freezer.

"One or two scoops?"

"What makes you think—" Mary Beth peeked around the corner of the freezer door and raised her eyebrow. "Five."

Mary Beth nodded in acknowledgement as she grabbed a bowl and spoon and scooped out three scoops of pistachio ice cream for her.

"This has to be about Lisa."

"I asked her to marry me," Sarah said as she scraped at a mound of ice cream.

"I take it she wasn't mad because you stole her idea."

"Not in the least."

Sarah reached to wipe a tear, but found none. It'd been years since she cried and she'd never been upset about a break-up. Maybe Lisa was right. Her friends were pairing off long term and suddenly the idea of dating for fun wasn't as appealing. Still no tears escaped, the only thing that told her she was in pain was a lump in her throat.

Mary Beth would be living with Eli if her Catholic guilt didn't make him go home each night. Gabbie was married. The only free one was Mandy, and she was just a ball of crazy right now. Half the time she spent around Mandy was to control an outburst.

Before she knew what happened Sarah's bowl was empty and Mary Beth was leaning against the breakfast bar holding her hands.

"What was I thinking?" Sarah asked.

"That you fell in love and wanted to give every bit of yourself to someone. Lisa's the one who lost in this, not you. You're going to come out of this better than you were when you entered the relationship."

"Is it stupid of me to think I can ever have a real family?"

"No. You're going to have a beautiful family someday, just not with Lisa."

"Maybe I should go after men."

"If you were Mandy I'd say yes, you should, but you've never felt comfortable with men that way. Ever. I don't even think you have ever had a boy crush?"

"God, I'm so gay. Aren't women supposed to be overly possessive in wanting a relationship?"

"I think some people want a family and some don't. It's not a guy/girl thing. Lisa's not that person."

"You know the worst part?"

"What?" Mary Beth said as she spooned the last of her ice cream in her mouth.

"I just want to curl up in her arms and have her tell me everything is going to be okay."

"I'd be worried if you didn't."

"God, she'll probably have her stuff out of the apartment by the time I'm back."

"What are you going to do?"

"I don't know. We renewed our lease in October. Actually, I renewed the lease. I should have seen this coming."

"Can you afford your place?"

"Not by myself."

"I know someone looking for a new apartment."

"Who?" Sarah asked, trepidatiously.

"Keep an open mind—"

"No."

"She's one of your best friends."

"I beg to differ."

"She's my sister."

"Technically you've only known that for less than six months."

"Technically she's been our best friend since we were seven."

"I hate you right now."

"It's only for a few months."

"She'll never say yes anyway. No woman will say yes to me, it seems."

"There you go, look on the bright side."

"Mandy," Sarah said with a sigh. "This day just keeps getting better and better."

* * * *

Karen Schroeder rubbed a tight muscle in her shoulder. The love hate relationship with her job wore on her body as much as it did her mind.

"I received an interesting call today," Howard Green said as he entered her legislative office in St. Paul, Minnesota.

Howard was an older man whose years of public service showed in his constantly stressed face and distended belly. He'd been a family friend of the Schroeders and had led more than one politician to the national stage.

"That was?" Karen replied as she flipped a page of the three hundred plus page bill in front of her and kicked off her heels under the desk quietly.

"At the Democratic Caucus a week ago, Congressman Chuck Johnson stepped down."

"He's not running? After twenty plus years? Let me guess, he thinks he can run against Senator Dunlap."

"Nope."

"It's a little late to throw his hat in for the Presidency," Karen noted with a little bit of interest. Howard wasn't one to bring random gossip into the office without good cause.

"He took a bribe."

She finally looked up from the legislation. "Really?"

"It's just now hitting the wires. Must be true because two days ago he played it off that Democrats needed new blood. We can use this scandal."

"We as in the Republican Party or we—"

"Team Schroeder. The call I got was the RNC. They've been watching you and think the new blood needed in the Fourth District is you."

"Me?" Karen reached for more than words as her skin erupted with goose bumps. Washington was always the end goal, but she expected a marathon, not a sprint. "I'm barely into my second term."

"There has been more than one successful President that ran after a few years in the Senate."

"Yes, but—"

"The national stage was always the goal, Karen. You're too good to just spend forty years in the State House."

"Isn't that the speech you gave me when you wanted me to get off the city council and run for Representative."

"It worked, didn't it?"

"I liked the city council," Karen replied meekly.

"And you like your current position, but politics is about advancing."

"I thought it was about serving the people."

"That's why you'll be the next U.S. Representative from the great state of Minnesota." Howard grinned like a dog at a butcher's window.

"The RNC really wants me?"

"We'll have to bury that one vote from last year, but yes, they're willing to help fund your campaign, contingent on you winning the primary in August."

Karen would have never guessed that the whole party would vote against the same-sex marriage amendment. She was sure at least a few would vote for it. The Democrats had all the votes they needed without her anyway, but her vote seemed to be all the news media could focus on for three days following the passing of the bill.

"What about Thompson?"

"Walter Thompson? He was the sacrificial lamb we were putting up for the Fourth District. He knows that."

"So I don't have to run against him in the primary?"

"Well…"

"Uh huh. That's what I thought." Karen leaned back in her chair and crossed her arms. "You want me to run against Thompson?"

"They tried to get him to step down."

"He wants the job."

"He can't win against Barbara Blake."

"Who?"

Howard pulled up his tablet and showed Karen his Google search. Barbara, aka Barbie, Blake was an up-and-coming community organizer. The write-ups in the *Strib* and *Pioneer Press* highlighted her raising funds for community centers and youth programs. Not to mention the community gardens and neighborhood watch groups. Yep, this woman had been planning a run for years. Karen had become cynical this last year as photo-ops took precedence over legislation too often for her taste.

"You're right," Karen sighed. Barbara was in the community where Walter was in the country clubs. Karen hadn't broken that inner circle enough. "I'm just getting a handle on this job."

"Karen, I'm telling you now and you can believe me sometime later, you're on the RNC's radar. You don't step up now, it may be ten or twenty years before you can make a move. This Blake lady could take the Democratic torch and roll with it. You grew up in the Fourth District. She moved there five years ago after graduating from the U."

Another calculated move.

"What do we have left in the war chest?"

"That's my girl," Howard exclaimed, and went into strategizing as if she'd just declared war on Thompson Street in Blakeville.

"Why do you do it?"

"What?"

"Run campaigns."

"I love the rush."

"Then why don't you run?"

"I hate politics." He winked and left the room.

Karen felt the same tingle she did every time she took a chance. The rush of excitement mixed with…she grabbed her wastepaper basket and proceeded to regurgitate her lunch. What the hell was she doing? She knew the plan. Get to the national stage, keep her district for a good six to ten years. Make her way onto the right committees, then, and only then, could she live the life she wanted. Until then, she'd keep up the appearance, even if it killed her inside.

Chapter Two

"In politics, if you want anything said, ask a man. If you want anything done, ask a woman."

—Margaret Thatcher

July

"Oh my God the way this guy IMs, I may need to buy stock in D batteries," Mandy said as she and Sarah walked through the displays at the Ramsey County fairgrounds "I'm thinking of flying out to Arizona next month, what do you think?"

Six months had passed since Mandy moved in, and Sarah had to admit living with her was entertaining.

"Is the goal of this excursion to be bound and gagged—"

"Yes please." Mandy jumped up and down while clapping her hands.

"I wasn't done," Sarah grumbled. "Raped and dropped into a shallow unmarked grave?"

"Why are you cock blocking me?"

"Why can't the mystery man come to you?"

"I'm sure he could," Mandy said as she absently twirled a lock of her jet black hair. "but then he'd have to research the best places in the Twin Cities to dump a body."

"I can see why he's hesitant."

"Exactly."

"For all you know he could be a sixty-year-old woman with a hankering for messing with young hotties."

"Aww, you're so sweet. Speaking of sweet, I need to get my funnel cake on."

Sarah shook her head as they headed closer to the rides where the food was, when a woman in red caught her eye. Saying that she stood out would be an understatement. This was a county fair where most people looked like she and Mandy did—hair half falling out of a ponytail, t-shirt clinging to the body from sweat, and shorts. Not Representative Karen Schroeder. Her auburn hair was pulled into a perfect French twist, and even though it was ninety-seven degrees, with humidity that made the air cling to everyone's skin, Karen Schroeder wasn't even sweating.

"Oh no, if I can't date a serial killer, you can't date a straight Republican," Mandy shook Sarah from her trance. "Unless you think she's family, just hiding out?"

"What do you know of family? You're barely a step-sister that only comes over on the holidays to eat."

"Because I don't discriminate like your hateful ass, you don't have to be mean."

"You're barely bi, so quit acting like you're all about the ladies. And I wasn't looking for a date. She's attractive. Am I not allowed to look at women at all now?"

"I've seen that look before. It was more than a mmm, let me get a piece of that. You get too invested in your conquests. You're always looking for your life partner or soul mate."

"What's wrong with looking for your soul mate? It's better than looking for your next infection."

"Again, it wasn't an infection."

"Then why did it take you the rest of the weekend before you could walk straight?" Mandy smiled and sighed. "Fine, if a man can screw you that well, why aren't you locking him down?"

"Because men like that don't get locked down. And really I wouldn't want that on the daily."

"Would you like information on the Representative?" an overly eager volunteer broke up the conversation with a pamphlet.

"Maybe," Mandy said with a smile that made Sarah instantly nervous.

"Don't," Sarah warned in a low tone.

"Oh, we're going to find out what the Rep's all about," Mandy said while batting her eyes. "Can I talk to her?"

"Of course," the bubbly girl said as she led them toward the put-together politician. "She's making the move to Congress. Representative Schroeder has done so much in the State House the last few years. She's who the Republican Party is looking for to take over the Fourth District."

"You'll have to tell me more. I'm a flake when it comes to elections," Mandy played innocent.

"Ramsey and part of Washington County is the Fourth District," Sarah said, stiffening her stance.

"Awesome, I was hoping Giggles here would tell me." Mandy glared at Sarah. At this point Sarah wished Mandy would entertain herself with Giggles and not take advantage of her slight crushing on the Rep.

"Representative Schroeder, these two women would like to know more about your platform," Giggles introduced the two of them.

Sarah suddenly had a problem breathing. Karen Schroeder was more than just put-together. She was breathtaking. Her high cheekbones and gentle, inviting eyes had Sarah envisioning things she shouldn't. Crushes on straight women had destroyed her in the past. Then again, this woman was a politician. She was in the spotlight. She was not a real person. Celebrity crushes were fine.

"What area are you most interested in?" she asked in a voice that wrapped around Sarah and cradled her.

"I'm kind of wondering about you as a person," Mandy said as she leaned on the table, squishing her full breasts together so they might as well be lighthouses on a foggy night. Even Sarah, who would never think of her best friend as a potential sexual partner, couldn't help staring.

"I'm an outdoors type, I love fishing at my parents' cabin," Karen said, not taking her eyes off Mandy's eyes. Damn, straight as an arrow. "Then again, when I'm not working, I just love being with my family. They're my anchor and guide me in my decisions."

"By family do you mean your husband and kids?"

"Oh, no, I barely have time for a personal life. My boyfriend and I—"

"That's too bad," Mandy purred and leaned over further. "Everyone needs a few minutes to snuggle in close with someone that gets what she desires."

"Excuse me?"

"You know what I mean." Mandy licked her lips, then bit her bottom one. "No matter what those desires are. Tell the truth, isn't there a little bit of you that wants to go behind the show barn with me right now?"

"I really don't know—"

"Excuse my friend," Sarah interjected as she pulled Mandy back from the table. "She has a brain tumor and can't control her sex drive."

"That's...strange...was she—" Karen started.

"I apologize for her making you uncomfortable."

"Is there a problem, sweetheart?" an attractive man wrapped a protective arm around Karen's shoulder.

"No, just backlash for my vote last year, I assume." Karen's inviting eyes became cold and hurt as she moved on to another constituent.

"What were you doing?"

"I wasn't being blatant. Only you got it. She's straight as hell or she would have been licking me as soon as I leaned over."

"Oh my God, Mandy, not everyone is like you."

"That was fun. Darn, we need to get to our booth before Gabbie blows a gasket. No funnel cake for me."

"Go get your funnel cake, I'll head to the booth."

"Love you, honey."

"Yeah, yeah." Sarah headed into the exhibition barn where they had a booth advertising the school of which she was part owner. When she reached the door of the barn, she turned back to get one last look of Representative Schroeder. She was smiling as she handed a man the same pamphlet Sarah was holding.

"Where's Mandy?" Mary Beth asked as Sarah pulled her polo over her t-shirt and redid her blonde ponytail. Gabbie must have already headed out.

"Funnel cake," she said, then under her breath mumbled. "And embarrassing me again."

"What?"

"Nothing, it's just sometimes I hate when she's right."

14

"It is painful."

"Her life is in shambles, but I wish I had her..." Sarah snapped her finger trying to come up with the word.

"Courage."

"Is that what it is?"

"Either that or strength. Think about it, her whole life she's been 'the bad one', 'the issue', the—"

"Unredeemable whore," Mandy interrupted, making Sarah and Mary Beth fall back into their booth. "I assume you're talking about me with those lead-ins."

She set down her plate of powdered and fried goodness.

"It's not what you think," Mary Beth began, but Mandy just shook her head and retrieved her polo from the hanger at the back of the booth.

"Right, because you're my big sister and love me more than anything," Mandy chided her recently anointed sister, Mary Beth. Nothing like finding out your best friend is also your sister, especially when your birthdays are only three months apart.

"Yes, I do love you," Mary Beth said as she tucked back Mandy's chestnut hair to reveal her hazel eyes with brown speckles. The hazel from their dad and the speckles from their mothers, Mary Beth's being green. "Sarah was just wishing she was as brave as you are."

With Mandy teetering on a manic episode, Sarah and her friends had been overly praising her lately to keep from a full blown meltdown.

"I'm not brave, I'm just not stupid enough to fall for someone who's completely unavailable."

"You told me anyone with a heartbeat was attainable last week," Sarah snipped.

"I was talking about my abilities, not yours."

"If I wanted the Rep I could get her."

"Could you now?" Mandy's right chestnut eyebrow popped into an arch.

"What, because she turned you down—"

"She did not turn me down, she publicly acted repulsed." Mandy plopped into the collapsible stadium chair behind their table. "Then she licked her lips."

"You said she was straight."

"For you, maybe, but I could turn that woman out in three—"

"Hello," Mary Beth stopped the conversation before it became NC-17 rated and engaged a young mother with three children. "You look like you're getting ready to go to school this fall."

The little girl with pigtails looked at Mary Beth, who'd taken a knee so she'd be eye level with the girl.

"No, I's only dis many," the girl said as she held up three fingers.

"Well, our school starts with kids that are that many."

The mother turned and eyed the booth. Sarah began explaining the Montessori Method and the idea of Children's House as Mary Beth and Mandy both engaged the two oldest children with an abacas and sand letters while the infant slept happily in the stroller.

"Mama look," the little girl squealed. "I writes my name."

Mandy had guided Abby with sand letters to not only spell her name, but do it in cursive. The sparkle in Mandy's eyes matched that of the girl's. Strange that Mandy could go from sex to nun in two point two seconds.

"Hello, I'm Amanda, the children usually call me Ms. Mand or Ms. Mandy. I'm the Children's House Director. I would be the one teaching Abby until she moved on to the Elementary One level with Sarah."

"Momma, can I go to school?" Abby asked, and the mother gave a worried look.

"Maybe, let me talk to the teachers some more."

"We've been teaching children for the past six years using this method. We just purchased an old St. Paul School building and this fall will be our first year there. Most of our students will be children that had attended our daycare center."

"Did you buy the old Lawson Elementary by Beaver Lake?"

"Yes."

"We live three blocks from there."

"It'd be a beautiful walk in the fall and spring."

"Look." The mother passed Sarah back the brochure on the school. "I can barely afford daycare, there's no way we could pay for private school."

"Don't let finances stop you." Sarah flipped open the brochure to the fourth page. "We're a new school, but we still qualify for all the grants that others do. Our Children's House students can read, write, and even do addition and subtraction with large numbers. Statistically, children that come from a Montessori school end up in the top ten percent academically. That's why we chose it as the platform for our daycare center."

"You said something about keeping your daycare center running."

"Yes, we've got an area that is connected, but separate for daycare. Some of our parents enjoy our service, but do not want us to become a school. This is the best of both worlds."

"And you'll have an instant feeder for those parents of younger kids."

"Yes." Sarah blushed at the obvious, yet not so obvious reason for maintaining the daycare center.

"Do you have a brochure on daycare fees?" she asked. "I'm assuming those aren't covered by financial aid."

"No, they're not, but you wouldn't be paying daycare for Abby, and Ben would be eligible for Children's House next year."

"You're a great sales woman."

"It's easy to sell something you believe in. I've seen the results in my partners Mary Beth and Gabbie's children. Mary Beth's son, Luke, is leaps and bounds ahead of the other kids in public school. Now he'll be able to attend our school and not be held back by students not at his level. Our daycare center portion is already open, feel free to come by and take a tour anytime."

The evening crowd in the exhibition barn thinned by seven as the rides at the midway lit up the skies. Sarah loved to watch the spinning rides as the sun set. She grabbed a quick brat and cheese curds, then returned to find Mandy straightening up their booth.

"I think we'll be having a lot of visitors over the next few days at the center," Sarah said as Mandy restocked a pile of brochures.

"I hope so, I love a small classroom, but I need another eight students at least."

"In three years we'll be making a third classroom at each level."

"You think so?"

"Yes. I've been getting interest from former customers that are now in the E two level. Yancy said she'd love to be the director if we get enough interest."

"We haven't had anyone in almost an hour, would you mind if I took off early?"

"No, just don't head to Arizona."

* * * *

Karen Schroeder was tired of the nasty comments that people made because she'd voted yes on the same sex marriage amendment. Then again, moving on to a Congressional seat, every crap she ever took would be up for examination. *Why Representative Schroeder, we see you enjoy corn, is that just in the summer time or all year long?* Why did she want to be in politics again...oh yeah, she was an idiot, that's right.

"You okay, Karen?" Ashton Gilmore asked when she finally got a break.

Ashton's cool blue eyes held nothing but love for her. Although others saw it as his undying devotion, they'd never know the devotion was purely platonic. It had to be. At one time, they'd tried to force it, and it had ended with a very embarrassing night for both of them. Best friends previously, Ashton and Karen were able to rebound quickly, and when she decided she wanted to be in public office, Ashton came with her to be her beard.

"I'm fine. Why do people feel the need to test me?"

"I think the brunette was looking out for the blonde."

"How is that?"

"I was at the four season porches display and happened to overhear them before Kimberly ambushed them."

"And?"

"The blonde was checking you out."

"Please..." Karen remembered the angelic face with a few strands of hair framing it from where they had escaped her ponytail. "She...really?"

"You're hot."

"You think she knew?"

"No, not in the least."

"Hmm..."

"I will get less ass if you come out, you know that, right."

"Who is it tonight?"

"Kimberly's been sniffing around, but there was a woman I thought would be a great envelope stuffer that left me her number."

"Why is it that people have no problem with you philandering around town as long as you're on my arm at political functions?"

"They all know you're the only one I'll ever love." He laid a sweet kiss on her forehead,

"And by love you mean cheat on religiously."

"Many a woman has genuflected to me."

"Have they now?" Karen shook her head. "Ash, do you think if I wasn't…"

"Gay as the day is long."

Ashton took her hands in his. She loved when someone just held her hands. The connection that came from shaking hands was violent and disingenuous to her. The gentle touch of a person just holding her hands could comfort her more than a warm blanket and a cup of soup on a February night.

"Yes."

"We could have been happy. Something tells me you could have satisfied me fully. Would you have taken my name?"

"With a hyphen," Karen joked, then got up and plopped in Ashton's lap, resting her head on his shoulder. "Maybe it's just you. You're too much like a brother."

"Okay," Ashton conceded as he brushed back her hair, then let his hand glide down her arm and come to rest on her hip. "That's a possibility. Of course, that doesn't explain Vonnie and Astrid."

"Nothing explains Astrid."

"Not even her breasts?"

"They were delicious," Karen sighed in remembrance. "And real. It's not fair that some women are born with tits like that. Ash…"

"It's your fault."

Karen gave him the scolding glare he always received when an erection popped up, especially when she'd been talking about her past lovers.

"Karen, you're attractive as hell. You can't expect me to not have this reaction when you discuss the flavor of another woman's body parts."

"Drop the porn image from your mind."

Ashton closed his eyes and sat silent for almost a minute.

"Nope, can't do it."

Karen got up from what had been a comfortable seat, let down her hair, and ran her fingers through it.

"I need to get some air," she said as Kimberly approached and she knew she could leave the booth.

"I need to call an envelope stuffer. See, it's your fault. If you'd just be normal

and—"

"Find you utterly irresistible."

"Most women do."

"Sorry, I got nothing happening here." Karen waved her hand from her breasts to her thighs. Nothing...and wasn't that the real tragedy?

"What was that Representative Schroeder?" Kimberly asked when she made it to the edge of the booth.

"There's nothing going on, we haven't had anyone since before you went on break. Would you mind closing up? I need to go stretch my legs."

"Sure, no problem."

Karen walked through the exhibition barn that had an amazing breeze blowing through it. Even where she'd been set up out on the main field there hadn't been this kind of wind. She guessed that was a good thing since their papers would have been flying.

She looked at the Extension Office info. A chiropractor had offered her a free assessment, which she took just for the two minute neck massage. She then saw some vendors selling homemade goods along with a few in-home businesses selling knives, spices, cookware, candles, and bags. All manned by women who were dreaming of a stay-at-home career.

When she turned the corner on the last row, she caught sight of the blonde from earlier in the day. Strange, she didn't picture her as a stay-at-home type. Karen made her way to the booth at the end of the aisle and saw learning tools. Not wanting to check out the blonde's ass, she read the banner on the top of the booth. She smirked at the language.

Growing Strong Montessori School. Where the leaders of tomorrow begin.

"Leaders of tomorrow, huh?" Karen asked, startling the young blonde who'd been organizing learning materials in the corner of the booth.

"That's what the sign says," she replied as she stood up and smoothed back the hair that had fallen from her ponytail. "I want to apologize again—"

Karen held up her hand. "No need. I've heard it all before and worse."

"Really, there's someone worse than Mandy?"

"I work in politics. She's a lightweight, and when you vote against your party, there is backlash sometimes."

"Vote against?"

"Isn't that why...Mandy, right?" the blonde nodded slowly. "Isn't that why Mandy came on to me? Because I must be a lesbian since I voted no which meant yes for same sex couples to marry?"

"We didn't know your voting record, and no, that wasn't the case. She was...you know what, it doesn't matter. But I am glad you voted no-yet-yes."

"You are?"

"Of course it ended my last relationship, but if I'm honest, it was over long before I made an ass of myself by asking my girlfriend to marry me."

"Ouch." Karen sat at the edge of the table and looked around the booth. "So you work at a Montessori School. I've never heard of that before."

"Montessori? It's a learning method. More about letting the children explore and learn on their own."

"On their own. Kids don't learn on their own."

"The inventors of Google did. Children are naturally curious. We feed that curiosity with learning tools."

"Okay, the first few grades maybe, but then—"

"Then the children have learned to ask questions. As the grades progress, we have guided learning, too, but the classroom is inviting to them. Things are at their level, not the teacher's."

21

"How long have you worked there?"

"My partners and I bought a daycare center seven years ago. We're finally at the stage of turning it into a school. We recently purchased a building, and as of September we have our first students."

Karen's heart pumped hard as she heard the woman explain her business, the plans, the hard work it must have been. Her blue eyes, though tired when Karen first arrived, were now alive and surrounded by blonde lashes and sun kissed skin.

"I'm Karen by the way," she said as she extended her hand. "I don't think we were properly introduced."

"You mean your first name isn't Representative?" the woman smiled and gently held Karen's hand. There was no firm I'm-sure-of-myself squeeze or awkward sweaty palm. It was soft, inviting, and had Karen stepping closer. "I'm Sarah, Sarah Lindstrom."

"It's very nice to meet you, Sarah. I hope you have a lot of success with your school." Karen didn't want to break the connection. She couldn't. Her hand stayed nestled in Sarah's as her lips began to tingle.

Sarah nervously wet her lips and Karen leaned closer, and then remembered her surroundings.

"I'm sorry," she said as she pulled away and moved to the other side of the table.

"You are...aren't you?" Sarah asked as her hands rested on the table in front of her.

"Are what?" Karen's breath quickened and the fear of outing herself came back. Her gut ached between her want and need to take Sarah in her arms and explore every inch, and throwing away everything she'd worked hard to construct.

"A closeted Republican."

Karen looked around to see if anyone was hearing their conversation. Sweat beaded on her forehead and the heat of the day finally hit her as her head swam.

"I've never heard it put that way," she finally replied when she'd convinced herself no one was listening. "Can I please sit in that chair?" she asked.

"Yes," Sarah said as she dug in a cooler under the table and fished out a cold bottle of water. "You okay?"

"I'll be fine," Karen assured as she took a drink from the bottle and felt the cold rush through her system. Fuck, fuck, fuck.

"I didn't mean to knock you off balance. It was...Mandy just...Mandy said I wasn't allowed to daydream about a straight Republican. I guess now I'll be allowed to have my fantasies."

The words rolled from Sarah's lips and sparked Karen into her own fantasies, her own desires. The ones she had to keep hidden from the world. Only a few women had touched her, and those women had something to lose, too. She dreamed of the day she could hold the woman she loved in public. Every day, going to work during the protests on the capitol steps, she caught herself looking longingly at the proud couples together. Then Ashton would take her hand and guide her to her office. Alone in there, she'd cry until she needed to have a brave face again.

"Who's the man candy you have protecting you?"

"I can't talk about this...here." She didn't know why she hesitated, but she wanted to tell Sarah more. She wanted to have Sarah in her life. It was a rush she'd never felt before, even with the other women.

"I've got twenty minutes before they close the doors and I can lock up." Sarah looked at her watch and let out a light laugh. "I know it sounds bad, but...will you meet me behind the barn at nine?"

Sarah was so sure of herself and who she was. Openly discussing a girlfriend without vetting Karen to make sure her secret wasn't going to hit the front page. A warmth tingled through Karen's core at the strength-of-self Sarah had to have and how that would translate in other areas.

"I...um...it's just—"

"You can't come out and play. I gotcha."

"It's not that. Anyone I'm with has to understand my belief system on ninety-nine percent of the platform is Republican. I need this to go no further than you and I."

"You haven't said anything, I have, and you've neither confirmed nor denied my accusations. Very good, Representative Schroeder." Sarah sat back and locked her eyes on Karen's. "But you caught my eye across a field where there were mini doughnuts, cheese curds, and funnel cakes. That's saying something. And we both know a few minutes ago you were less than an inch from kissing me. That says something, too."

* * * *

Holy. Shit. Sarah tried to not come on too strong, but Karen's light caramel eyes with auburn hair circling her face made it hard to keep her distance. Karen was beautiful and smart with only one little flaw.

Why was Sarah even thinking that way? Lisa may have been right—she was looking to pair up, but she couldn't do that with Karen no matter how much she wanted to. Karen was in the closet, something Sarah never had to deal with. Her family outed her before she really understood her feelings. In her house, everything was discussed. She never knew that didn't happen at most houses until she spent the night at her friends and saw the immediate wall for 'inappropriate' topics.

"Yes," Karen said under her breath. The break in silence caught Sarah off guard. "Yes it does, but you have to promise me that you won't tell."

"Tell what? That I got to talk to my State Representative about education funding for private schools?"

Karen gave a half-hearted smirk.

"I'm nothing if not devoted to my constituents."

Sarah finished closing up at the booth and said goodbye to the man from The Mad Scientist in the booth next to them. He'd be of use later in the year with a great 'going out' opportunity for the kids in her class. He may even help her with a few demonstrations if they had enough money in the discretionary fund.

Her stomach was a bundle of nerves and she wished she hadn't eaten as much grease as she had that day. She'd snagged the last bottle of water so she had something to fumble with in her hands, and when she went around the back of the old barn, Karen turned and smiled at her. It was a cloudless night and the stars in the dark area behind the barn shone brightly. What was she thinking? Meeting a woman she just met in a dark area with no protection? But then again, Karen was in more danger than she was.

"Where are the secret service agents?"

"I'm still small potatoes. I don't even get a state trooper."

"Tell me again about the man."

"Man? Oh you mean Ashton, my *boyfriend*," the words rolled off her tongue with more sarcasm than Sarah expected. "You have any brothers?"

"Yes, one older one."

"He's my unrelated one. He plays the part at major functions."

"And he knows?" Sarah stepped closer to Karen and the heat from her body surrounded Sarah in such a way she couldn't help being drawn in closer.

"At one time, he tried to cure me."

"That sounds painful. Did it involve a voodoo priestess?"

"You got the priest right," Karen said with a slight giggle. "No, actually he's decided if I'm not turned on by him, no man could turn me on."

"A little full of himself, isn't he?"

"Yes, but I've yet to see the woman who could resist him."

"You're looking at one," Sarah said and caught a few strands of Karen's hair. "You on the other hand…"

Sarah curled the long auburn hair around her finger. She wanted to taste Karen's lips, to be close enough to share the same air. She needed to feel more than the warmth of her body, she needed to feel Karen's curves against hers.

When Karen pulled in her lips, then released, and a flash of red glistened from being wetted, Sarah could no longer resist. Her lips found Karen's and the sweet taste made Sarah's head dizzy. When Karen's tongue licked at Sarah's, she crushed herself against Karen's body.

The touch was exhilarating. Even if it could go no further than this, Sarah reveled in the idea that for one moment she'd felt a woman who seemed to want her as much as she wanted them.

Karen's hand went to Sarah's belly and tugged at her shirt. Goosebumps erupted from her touch as Karen's soft hand slid across Sarah's bare stomach.

Love me. Love me. Love me. Thoughts raced through Sarah's mind, and she wanted to suppress the voices, but they became overwhelming. Karen's hand moved and cupped Sarah's breast, kneading the flesh while her tongue stroked Sarah's.

"We have to stop," Karen gasped, removed her hand from under

Sarah's shirt, and tightly wound her arms around Sarah. "You're going to ruin me."

Chapter Three

"I am good, but not an angel. I do sin, but I am not the devil. I am just a small girl in a big world trying to find someone to love."
—Marilyn Monroe

The door to Mandy's room opened and Sarah turned with a plate of pancakes and a smile. "Guess who is family..." she began, and then saw what could only be described as a Carney. The man had what might be considered an attractive smile and blue eyes if he wasn't so covered in about two days' worth of beard growth. His toothy grin made her understand Mandy must have just picked the one with the least amount of cavities and the most teeth. "And you are?"

"He's Bobby," Mandy said as she stumbled from her room. "Mmm...you made me pancakes."

"I don't know why." Sarah grumbled.

"You got some of those for me, too?" Bobby's slight Southern accent completed the package of circus folk stereotypes.

"Yeah, sure."

"So our little congresswoman wasn't offended by my advances." Mandy smiled as she cut into the pancakes.

"Yes, she was, but not for the initially conceived reasons."

"You're related to a congresswoman?" Bobby asked.

"No," Mandy said while swallowing. "She means in the family of women."

"I don't get it."

"Sarah here prefers the ladies."

Sarah arched her eyebrow at Mandy.

"Let me ask you something," Bobby began and Sarah stifled her growl. "Now every woman needs dick once in a while..." Seriously? This jackass was really going to go there. "Now I know I've been in a few ménages in my day—"

"You mean you allowed a girl in with you and another guy because every once in a while you need a little pussy instead of a dick up your ass," Sarah snapped, and Mandy practically choked on her food.

"Look, all I'm asking is do you and your woman do it all at once with the guy or do you go off on your own?"

"You brought this into my home," Sarah growled at Mandy.

"Well," Bobby said as his eyebrows knitted together. "I...I was just gonna say Mandy's got my number—"

"No, I don't," she said quickly.

"Oh, it's—"

"Stop." Mandy pointed her fork at him and began to spin it in a circle. "You ran out of tickets there, big man, no more rides for you."

"Why you gotta be a bitch about it?"

"Why are you acting like this is going past pancakes?" Mandy asked with no interest in the response. "And I didn't even make the pancakes. My domestic here did."

Sarah would have normally smacked Mandy, but she was too busy holding back her laughter. Mandy was more of a man than any woman she ever knew. She slept with who she wanted, when she wanted, and kept them around for as long as she wanted. Her partners never had a chance. Sarah wished she could have that kind of separation when it came to sex, but alas she was a girly girl deep down.

"What are you sayin'?"

"I'm saying get ready because we both need to head back to the fair. Also, I have to discuss some things with my girl, so leave."

"I needed another shower anyway." Bobby left in a huff to the bathroom.

"Again?" Sarah tried to stifle the image of dirt washed down her drain or worse yet, creating a ring in her tub.

"Like I was going to sleep with him before he washed off two days of fair sweat. What kinda girl do you think I am?"

"Someone who doesn't know you don't bring Carneys home. Are

you crazy? You feed them and they come back."

"Not the way he eats," Mandy replied flippantly.

"That explains the fact I actually thought you were asleep when I got home."

"Silly fool. If I'm not up watching bad reality TV, I'm getting me some."

"How much sex do you have?"

"Don't look at me like that. I never said I was always with someone."

Sarah shook her head to clear it like an etch-a-sketch. "You told old Billy Bob there you had to talk to me."

"Oh, yeah." Mandy went back into the kitchen and picked two more pancakes off Sarah's warming plate and returned to her seat. "Your politician, I don't see her doing the walk of the Carney this morning."

"I'm not really a sex-on-the-first-date type of girl."

"A date? I'm impressed."

"Not really, just a secret meeting. Shit. You can't tell anyone she's gay."

"Um, the only people I'd tell are the two you're going to tell as you gush about her."

"I'm not going to gush about her. It was just one kiss and a nice conversation."

"And you're already keeping, yet not keeping, a secret that could potentially ruin her life."

That hit Sarah like a ton of bricks. She'd never kept things from her friends. They were her closest companions and most trusted confidants. There had never been jealousy or petty fights over boys growing up. No one was jealous of what the other had. Even Mandy, who didn't have a father growing up and lived in apartments when the rest of them lived in homes with yards and even pets.

"She must assume that I'd tell you."

"Why would she assume that?"

"I have friends, she must know that, and a family, if we're going to start dating—"

"She's a politician in a party that bans benefits for LGBT groups left and right. I was serious when I said you shouldn't date her. Fuck her,

29

sure, but date, no. She'll break your heart because if she doesn't love herself, how can she love you?"

"Who's talking love?"

"We're talking about you and a woman. You don't have anonymous sex for fun and orgasms."

"Well…" Sarah became indignant until she had to admit Mandy was right. She didn't know how to be casual with a lover. Or even take a lover. "What if I want to? Can you teach me?"

"Teach you?" Mandy said the words slowly. "Um…you're past that stage of your life."

"I can still learn."

"It's not something you can teach."

"Why not?"

"Because you're past the age of three. Come on, you took the same classes I did. It's a personality thing. You weren't raised in the Rockwell-esque family Mary Beth was, but you had consistent family members. People didn't come in and out of your life. I had to enjoy the few minutes I got with a person. Outside of you guys, no one was guaranteed to be there for me growing up."

Sarah never thought of Mandy as a deep thinker, but she'd really examined herself.

"Honey, I love you to death, but you can't have one night stands because you expect the person to be there in the morning."

"Bobby's here."

"If he had a car and I hadn't fallen asleep, he'd be in a RV at the fairgrounds."

"Do you like when a guy stays over?"

"Usually with guys I'm fine, but never with women."

"Because women are clingy."

"Isn't there some stupid mating hormone that releases during sex? Women tend to nest. I mean it's my house, who wakes up and makes breakfast in a stranger's home?"

"But you had sex with them, they're not strangers."

"I don't know Bobby's last name. His birthday. Or if he's married nor do I care to find out. He's a stranger."

"We need to talk about the married part."

30

"Whatever," Mandy said as she waved her hand. "What time do we need to be at the fair?"

"Nine."

"I'm gonna hop in the shower quickly. You good?"

"Yeah, I showered last night."

"Good. Well, I guess Bobby gets one more look at my sexy ass."

* * * *

The last day of the fair arrived, and with over a thousand new names added to Karen's mailing list, it was deemed a success, but there was one name and number she'd been thinking about since the night before. She feared telling Ashton about what happened, but inside she was bursting to discuss the possibility of making a relationship work. Then again, it was the wrong time to even think about anything but the primary and the debate less than a month away.

"The polls put you up fifteen points over Thompson," Howard said as he pulled Karen aside.

Although it was a warm July morning and a Sunday to boot, Howard was still in a button-up shirt and dress pants.

"I told you this glad handing would pay off."

"Do I have to do the Washington County Fair, too?"

"Yes, and the State Fair."

"Eleven days?"

"It's the great Minnesota get together. Once you beat Thompson you'll need to get out there."

"How much will I have to be there?"

"A few hours every day. You'll get some photo-ops with the Butter Queen. Maybe stop by a barn, catch a show at the Grandstand."

"Eat corn on the cob and Sweet Martha's cookies and drink a glass of cold milk."

"While going down the giant slide."

"You know I do have a job to do."

"The state house doesn't have anything pressing for the next few months." Howard eyed Karen with a knowing look. "What's going on, Peanut?"

As someone who'd known her since she was in diapers, he was the one person outside of her immediate family who could call her that. He also knew more about her than her parents did when it came to her personal life. It was his job to know what could come out and how to camouflage behavior and people.

"I met someone."

"How much has happened?"

Karen's face flushed remembering the feel of Sarah's bare flesh.

"How much?" Howard growled.

"Oh, not that," she scoffed and crossed her arms. "A kiss, that's it. I didn't even confirm my preference." She kept her face as straight as she could.

"Was there tongue? That kinda confirms it. Something tells me you didn't just give a peck on the cheek."

"That's none of your business."

"I'm not asking for video confirmation, but we both know it is my business. I need to know who you, Ashton, and every other politician I work for sleeps with, unless it's your spouse."

"You can actually keep up with who Ash sleeps with?"

"Don't change the subject."

"I'm just saying that's impressive."

"He doesn't care about them. I have a form for them to sign..." Howard shook his head and returned to the subject at hand. "Who is she?"

"A teacher I met yesterday."

"You got into a detailed budgetary spending debate?"

"Not really." Karen could feel the teenage her coming back as she rocked back on her heels. "Howard, I like her. I want to get to know her."

"Can she join the staff?"

"No, she is not that type of person."

"All teachers are political."

"I don't want her on the campaign."

"Now I'm interested. Why not?" Howard lowered his eyes at Karen and she felt like she'd been scolded.

"That *is* none of your business."

"Karen—"

"Representative," Karen snipped. Sure he'd known her since diapers, but she still deserved the respect her office afforded her.

"You want to go there. Fine, Representative Schroeder, I don't care that you like to fuck women, but the voters in the party you ascribe to do. You need to accept the fact that you are at a point in your career…"

Howard's voice faded out as he continued the same speech he'd given her a half dozen times. Not because she knew it, but because Sarah was walking by with Mandy. She caught Karen's eye and gave a small smile to which Mandy backhanded her.

Karen guessed they were both being told it was a mistake to be together. What she hadn't told Howard was she couldn't control herself around Sarah. That's why Sarah could never be her little secret on the campaign. Sure she'd played off hugs or hand holding with Astrid as one woman consoling another or some such thing, but with Sarah she wanted to feel and touch everything.

"Are you even listening to me?" Howard snapped.

"It's all you can do to promise the party I'll vote their way after my blatant disregard to policy concerning the marriage amendment. The last thing you need is for me to come out right now."

"You didn't hear a word I said."

"Was it a different speech from the last five you gave me?"

"Yes, this time I said if you can't control your urges—"

"I'd have to start over as a Democrat and give my parents a stroke."

"Your mother gets the stroke, your dad would have a massive coronary."

"As long as they go out together."

"Is this part of your 'family first' thing?"

Karen rolled her eyes and attempted to put on her game face, but failed because all she wanted to do was visit the exhibition barn.

"Representative." Kimberly poked her head around the screen they'd put up to cover their booth.

"Yes," Karen replied and swallowed hard.

"I have a few people that would like to meet you. I think they'd be big contributors."

"Well, I'd hate to have Howard become a volunteer that had to believe in me no matter what, so I better smile and say hi."

33

"Not funny."

"What?" Karen said with her palms up as she shrugged.

Karen helped sign up new volunteers and even sold a few tickets to her next fundraiser. By lunch she was starving and had to step away. Her hands hurt and she was happy her parents would be there by two to help out. In line for a pulled pork sandwich, Sarah was talking with a redhead. Karen approached and stood behind the two of them for a moment.

"I don't know, I'm sure we'll get the numbers up in the E1 level by winter break. I'd love to have another five students, but looking at the number of Children's House five-year-olds I might be over run next year," Sarah said.

"I'd rather be turning kids away than having to struggle to keep the lights on," the other woman said. "About that."

"What," Sarah whined. "Please don't tell me I'll need another roommate. I thought business owners were supposed to have money."

"We're doing good, but I'm worried because one of the grants we earned lost its federal funding."

"Not the big one?"

"I haven't committed suicide yet, so no, but it was the one for supplies and employee increases. Fifty thousand renewable for five years."

"What fund did it come out of?" Karen interrupted before she realized it proved she had been eavesdropping. "I'm sorry, none of my business."

"You're in my district," Sarah said with a smile. "What's the point of voting if I can't talk directly with my Representative?"

"Um..." the redhead said. "Why do I feel like I'm missing something?"

"I'm Representative Karen Schroeder and I'm running for Congress in the Fourth District. Although I'm in the State House now, I'd love to help if I could. Sarah told me a little about your school last night."

"Did she now?" the redhead eyed Sarah, then turned and smiled. "I'm Mary Beth Wallace, the business end of the Growing Strong Mafia."

"Can I take your order?" the tired food worker asked. They all ordered, and then headed to a picnic table.

"I don't know what fund it came out of," Mary Beth confessed as they got settled. "It was the Education Alternatives Grant. Since our school is not traditional, we qualified."

"What were the criteria?"

"Newly formed school. We'd have to show growth in student body and testing."

"Have you looked at Women's Venture? They have all sorts of grants for women run companies. Are you at least fifty percent female in upper management?"

"We're a hundred," Sarah said as her blue eyes told more than her comments did. Karen squirmed in her seat at the way Sarah's lips formed the words. A hundred percent woman would describe her.

"All my fault I must confess," Mary Beth said. "I guess Sarah didn't get into the dirty details of how we started."

"No, she didn't. She also didn't explain the mafia?"

The two women burst into laughter.

"It's a nickname we picked up a year ago. Gabbie Thomas, one of our partners, met and married a man who gave us the nickname The Growing Strong Mafia."

"How did you earn it?"

"He says the four of us are like family. We fight with each other, but if anyone crosses one of us, then they have to face the wrath."

"What did he do to Gabbie?"

"Nothing, he's no fool." Sarah smiled and exchanged glances with Mary Beth.

"I promised Luke he could go through the fun maze after lunch," Mary Beth excused herself. "Please tell Sarah about any other grants or funding you may know about, we could really use them."

"Does she know?" Karen asked when Mary Beth was out of earshot.

"Nope."

"Then why did she leave so abruptly?"

"She probably suspects." Sarah sipped on her drink. "The four of us have been friends since first grade. Mary Beth and I have known each other for as long as I can remember. My family lived next door to her for a few years before they moved two blocks away."

"Would she say anything?"

Michel Prince

"To who?"

"Anyone."

Sarah sighed and rested her head on her upturned palm. "I enjoyed last night."

"How can you be like that?"

"Like what?"

"Out there."

"It's only hard not being yourself." Sarah took Karen's right hand in hers and a shiver shot down Karen's spine. "Like this, I'd love to hold your hand right now, but instead I have to inspect your beautiful ring so people around us don't know."

Sarah looked into Karen's eyes as if she were willing her to do more than explain her ring. Her hand was gentle and delicate against Karen's and she couldn't help wishing this would never end.

"It was a gift from my parents on my sixteenth birthday."

"Was it now?"

Sarah turned Karen's hand from side to side and the light caught the sapphire, shooting blue rays from the precious stone. Karen didn't want to break the connection from Sarah's touch even though she knew she had to. They'd been holding hands for too long. Touching in a way that could be misconstrued. Then again, Karen wasn't a hundred percent sure it would be wrong because her belly was churning and she knew what she wanted. She just wasn't sure if she could give up everything for a woman who would probably abandon her. Sarah pulled back her hand and Karen felt a cold chill shoot up her forearm.

"Now, if we weren't pretending I could have held your hand even after we got up. I could have held it as I walked you back to your booth on the way to mine. My fingers could have brushed back those few strands of hair that fell over your face so I could take in your eyes. Then my hand, that just a few moments ago held yours, could cradle your cheek until my lips met yours."

Karen brushed back her hair and inhaled sharply.

"Instead, I'll take my leave."

"Wait." Karen reached for Sarah's arm.

"Careful," Sarah warned, looking at Karen's long fingers curled around her forearm. "People might start to talk."

36

"About a friend stopping another, I don't think so. I've been playing this game long enough." Karen stood and let her hand slide down Sarah's arm until their fingers lightly curled, then released. "I'll be done by five. I don't need to clean up. How about real food tonight?"

"My cholesterol numbers haven't hit myocardial infarction level yet," Sarah said with a smirk.

"I could get extra cheese on a pizza," Karen suggested.

"Maybe a bottle of wine?"

"I could meet you by seven. I'd like to shower."

"Where would we meet?"

Karen then rocked back on her heels and saw a bigger problem. Where could they go and not be suspect?

"Um...well..."

"How about my apartment?" Sarah offered, and then took her phone out of her back pocket. "Here, type in your phone number and I'll text you my address."

"How about I just enter in my GPS on my phone? It'll save me a step."

"Or you won't have to explain why my number's on your phone."

"I'll be happy to add your number to my phone." Karen inhaled sharply. "When I know you're worth the risk."

"Is this a good in bed thing—"

"No," Karen replied sharply as three emotions tore through her. The first was desire in its most animalistic form, as images of discovering the soft feel of Sarah's skin in the most intimate of ways. The second and strongest one was the visceral reaction that Sarah could even think that was Karen's only desire...then the images swirled and shame took over.

"Too bad." Sarah smiled. "At least then I would have known my number would make it into your phone."

Chapter Four

"I did then what I knew how to do. Now that I know better, I do better."
—Mayo Angelou

Mandy must have been rubbing off on Sarah, and as much as the little voice in her head yelled to stop, she couldn't. She had learned the rush of the tease. To see a face blush, eyes turn down, and the best was the nibbling on the lips. Who knew turning on someone else could get the teaser just as tweaked?

After giving Karen directions, Sarah practically skipped back to the booth, and when she saw Mandy's dark head of hair she grabbed her from behind and declared "I love you."

"Excuse me?" a stranger blurted as Sarah fell back into the booth with apologies.

"I thought you were someone else."

Mandy had been around the corner buying homemade caramels when she returned to the booth and burst out laughing.

"I'm so sorry, ma'am," Mandy said as she rested her hand on the woman's forearm. "She didn't grab your boob, did she?"

"What...I..." The flustered woman stumbled.

"She usually does when she's like this. Boob then ass, I can't take her anywhere."

"I apologize," Sarah's mortified voice came out as a croak barely heard.

The woman walked away in a huff. Mandy put her right hand on her hip and smirked.

"Something you want to share with the group?"

"Not really." Sarah retreated again and flopped into the stadium chair.

"What's going on? Something tells me I want to skip my lunch break." Gabbie Thomas sat next to Sarah. Gabbie's raven-haired ponytail came out of her Green Fightin' Sioux Basketball hat while her grey eyes looked at Sarah with a knowing look.

"No."

"You hugged Mandy. You never hug Mandy."

"You haven't been in my apartment late at night. We snuggle all the time."

Gabbie looked from Sarah to Mandy, who still had her hand on her hip.

"I want details."

"I honestly have no idea," Mandy replied, unrolled another piece of caramel, and popped it into her mouth. Through the chewy treat she asked what Sarah assumed was, "You wanna enlighten me?"

"You're a good influence on me."

"Am I now?" Mandy crossed her arms. "Is this one of those let's-build-Mandy-up-so-she-doesn't-crack comments?"

"Nope, not this time."

"How did I influence you positively then?"

"I've learned the art of the tease."

"The Rep?"

"You would have been proud of me."

"Who's the Rep?" Gabbie asked.

Mandy and Sarah both looked around at the people passing, then Mandy leaned in and whispered in Gabbie's ear.

"No. Frickin'. Way." Gabbie exclaimed. "You have a crush," she gushed.

"Crushes are for teenagers."

"It's about time you became a teenager. So I assume something good happened?"

"Yes, but I'm not supposed to tell anyone and now I've blurted...how do closeted people do it? I couldn't imagine not telling my best friends or family about someone that makes me this excited."

"Is it just her body?" Gabbie teased. "Then I would know Mandy controlled you."

"No, she's smart and funny…and I need the apartment to myself tonight."

"Is the Real Former Great Dancers of the Trailer Park on tonight?"

"I hope to not find out."

"Wanton trollop," Mandy teased.

"Ugh, you guys have your own language now," Gabbie whined. "I need some girl time before I'm sucked into the toddler world forever."

"I don't think a night of drinking and debauchery is what you need." Mandy winked.

"No," Sarah gasped at the news. Sure, she and Mandy had a short hand, but there were a few things they all knew.

"It's early, really early."

"Oh my God, a mafia member's having a baby in wedlock."

"Shut up."

Sarah placed her hand on Gabbie's belly that didn't show any signs, but she couldn't be happier for her friend. Although Gabbie and her husband Case adopted his now three-and-a-half-year-old siblings Claire and Charlie, Case's nerves about infertility being genetic had the two of them trying to get pregnant.

"You're gonna have a Buddha belly."

"A fat ass and big boobs."

"And the cutest little mocha skinned baby with curly hair."

"Claire is going to freak out." Gabbie sighed.

"Oh yeah, she might end up fighting you to be the mommy."

The day progressed and of course Mary Beth learned of the secret they all had to keep. Being sweet, they let Sarah go home early and she rushed to tidy up her apartment and take her own shower. When she opened the door at seven, she was shocked to see not only Karen, but Ashton, too.

"Am I missing something?"

"Karen was being followed by a few reporters," Ashton started. "So I get to eat on the couch while you two have your intimate dinner."

Not very intimate with a guy in the room.

"Can we come in before they figure out which apartment I'm coming to?" Karen pleaded.

"Right." Sarah stepped to the side and extended her arm to usher them in.

Karen placed two pizzas on the counter and smiled at Sarah.

"I'll get the plates," Sarah said and opened her cupboards. Irritation began at the top of her forehead and worked its way across the back of her head to her spine. Was this the nineteen sixties and she and Karen Rock Hudson and Cary Grant? No, they didn't have a woman with them. They had a third guy for a guys' night out.

"Are you mad? If so we can leave."

"Why? So a reporter can think you're delivering to shut-ins?"

Ashton laughed and flopped on her couch.

"What are we looking at for TV? Dish? Cable? Premium channels?"

"Cable, two movie channels. This something you two do a lot?"

"She just accused you of being a slut." Ashton snapped his head back to look at them. "I like her."

"Because you're not the slut this time?" Karen mused.

"Pretty much."

"I thought the reason we were at my apartment is so we could be together and not threaten your image."

"I won't tell." Ashton flipped on the TV.

"And be alone."

"I won't peek either," Ashton assured with a cocked eyebrow.

Wrapping her arms around Sarah's neck, Karen stepped toward her. Her soft scent and warmth weakened Sarah's resolve as their foreheads gently rested against each other.

"I promise," Karen began, as Sarah became lost in her caramel eyes, "That you and I will be alone. I want to know about you. I'm not trying to be presumptuous, but what do you say to you and me curling up on your bed…"

Sarah began to protest, Karen pulled her closer, and their lips met. Not a deep, passionate kiss. An assuring peck that had Sarah wanting more. She pulled her lips in after Karen released her to taste whatever bit of her was still there.

Karen's hands glided down Sarah's arms and came to rest on her hips.

"I just want to talk," she said quietly, then raised her voice. "And someone tends to butt in."

"G rated pillow fight, I swear it hasn't gone beyond that," Ashton called from the couch without turning around.

"Do I want to know?" Sarah asked.

"Unless we get him a woman to distract his mind…it wanders. He's a man."

"You noticed, I'm touched, of course that means I'm disgusting because I can't keep my sexual organs tucked away."

"Now I see why you want to be in another room," Sarah said, then ran her fingers through Karen's luxurious auburn hair. "I'll grab the wine. My room's right there."

"I'd kiss you, but…"

They both looked at Ashton, who was now more interested in them than the TV, and sighed.

"You promised me there would be perks to being your man candy," Ashton whined as he crossed his arms and stretched out.

"How much do you make being an 'advisor' in my office?" Karen asked with air quotes.

"Blah, blah."

As they stepped into Sarah's bedroom she trembled. Outside of Mandy stealing clean khakis in the morning, she hadn't had anyone but Lisa in here. Her queen size bed was big enough that they could have a little picnic and keep their distance, even if that wasn't what she wanted to do.

She wanted to learn about Karen from forehead to toes. She wanted to spend hours exploring her soft curves and tasting her flesh. She wanted to have her bunching up the sheets in her fingers as her body flushed from an orgasm that would make her proud to hold Sarah's hand in public.

Sarah instantly plopped on the bed and crossed her legs.

"I'm not someone who holds back on much."

"That's probably why I'm so attracted to you," Karen confessed as she placed the pizza box between the two of them.

Sarah poured a glass of *Barefoot* Merlot and watched as the red liquid swished in the glass. Swirling the wine in the goblet, her eyes stayed focused on the motion, trying to find the words she needed to say.

Physically, Karen had her body rushing like she'd never known, but who was the real person? The one on the campaign trail who stays silent on issues that would affect her personally, or the one who wanted to find out more about her? And could Sarah ever trust someone who lives two lives?

"Have you become hypnotized?"

"What?" Sarah asked around a swallow of the sweet wine.

"You kinda checked out on me."

"Did I?" Sarah sighed. "I'm just not sure what we have in common."

"You mean beside the fact neither of us can look away when we see the other?"

"Yeah," Sarah said as she looked up and knew exactly what Karen meant. Damn it.

"I'm loyal as hell to the people I love," Karen began. "That's probably why I haven't come out yet. My parents have this idea of me…my campaign manager likes to remind me my mother would have a stroke and my father a coronary."

"If they love you—"

"How old were you when you told your parents?"

"I never really told them, they just knew."

"You never had to sit there scared with your stomach in knots? Or your heart full of pain because you found someone? Keeping your eyes down, afraid they'd see the desire in your eyes for the girl sitting across from you at a table?"

"No more than anyone else I guess. I came home and my mom just saw on my face that I'd met someone. She did the same thing when my brother or sister had their first love." Sarah smiled in remembrance. "I guess I was a little nervous, but she looked at me and said 'okay, who is she'?"

"What if she would have said 'he' instead?"

"I might have been nervous, but me saying 'Kayla' seemed so natural to both of us."

"I couldn't imagine that. My mother's been hooking me up with boys since I was two. 'Oh is he your boyfriend'? I know all parents do that, but once…I think I was five or six and playing house with my friend Olivia…there weren't any boys around and they weren't going to

43

play house anyway. I said we had two mommies in the house." Karen shuddered. "That was the last time I made that mistake. Next time one of us was the daughter."

"I'm sorry."

Karen tipped back some wine of her own. "I thought we were supposed to be talking about each other."

"I think this is more telling than you explaining your feelings on the debt ceiling."

"I'm more than politics you know."

"Are you? Let me guess, you play classical piano and a mean game of canasta?"

"Violin and poker."

"Well, well Representative." Sarah smirked. "Do you bowl, too? I might just fall in love."

"I have a two-sixty average."

"Are you sure your family doesn't think you're gay?"

They spent the next half hour eating pizza, sharing fair horror stories, and laughing at some of the craziness. Karen had a light laugh, but with her sense of humor it was quite infectious. She was the oldest in a family of five, all girls. She was the only one not married, even Karen's twenty-year-old sister Darlene had been married earlier this year. Although all the Schroeder girls were successful in one way or another, Karen, the politician, was the beacon to which they were all measured. If only Ashton would make an honest woman of her. Only a handful of people knew her true nature—Howard, her campaign manager, Ashton, two former girlfriends, and now Sarah.

"I have a confession to make," Sarah said.

"What's that?"

"My friends know."

"Your friends know what?" A low grumble came from Karen as her face paled.

"They won't say anything I swear."

"Why would you tell them?"

"Because I..." Sarah didn't want to become defensive, just hold to her resolve. She shouldn't have told her friends, not until she was sure there was something really to tell, but damn it... "Because I couldn't stop thinking about you. I was glowing remembering your kiss. And…"

Sarah stumbled to find the words, but she wasn't going to apologize. That she refused to do.

"My friends could read my face."

"What did it say?" Karen asked with a strained whisper.

Cradling Karen's smooth cheek in her hand, Sarah felt the draw pulling her in, and they locked eyes as their faces came within a breath of each other.

"I met someone that with one kiss changed the way I see the world."

Karen captured Sarah's lips and stroked back her blonde hair. Straddling Sarah's hips Karen deepened the kiss, and when their tongues touched, Sarah moaned. They fell into a kiss Sarah had never experienced, hungry and wanton. As if neither of them could stop. Her lips tingled and electricity seemed to surge over her skin. Karen pulled at the hem of Sarah's shirt and their kiss broke as her vision was lost in a blue whirlwind and her shirt hit the floor.

"I want to taste every inch of you." Karen was no longer the prim and proper politician. Her normally caramel eyes became deep brown with desire. The summer tan she sported was flushing crimson across her cheeks. "Please don't tell me no. Everyone tells me I can't have what I want."

The hormones rushing through Sarah's system were conflicting with her brain that said Karen denied herself. Then again, Sarah never had someone tell her that being herself wasn't right. She wasn't supposed to deny the feelings inside. She was to embrace them as long as she was happy. Sure, she'd had heartbreak, but she never hid who she was. In this room, right now, the only world that mattered was the world she and Karen had created, and in that world Karen could be true to herself. Sarah wanted to give her that. She wanted to show Karen that who and what she was would never be wrong in her eyes.

Bringing her hands behind her back, Sarah unlatched her bra and let the restraint fall to the floor.

* * * *

There is something about a woman truly giving themselves to another person that makes their body react and give off signals to all five senses. At this moment in time, Sarah's body might as well have whispered in Karen's ear of the pleasure it yearned for. It glowed before her eyes from the blood rushing to and darkening her nipples. It smelled of desire as pheromones filled the air. It felt warm, soft, and supple, even with goose bumps erupting wherever Karen's fingers teased…but it was the taste Karen needed. The taste that told her Sarah would be hers completely for as long as they had. Whether it be a minute, an hour, a day, or a lifetime.

Karen hoped her fear could dissipate long enough for Sarah to see the same signals coming from her. From the first taste of Sarah's lips, Karen knew the weight she'd carried needed to be let go. She couldn't hide who she was and also be with who she wanted, no, needed. She needed to be with Sarah for her own sanity.

Eating pizza and hiding in a back bedroom never seemed bad until she saw the disappointment in the most beautiful blue eyes she'd ever seen. Sarah had already conceded and allowed them to meet in private, twice, but to be hidden like she was a pariah wounded her and Karen couldn't let her be hurt. Not this time and not to this woman.

The sweet taste from the wine still nicely covered Sarah's lips as Karen captured them. Her fingers tangled in the long, blonde hair as her own lips tingled, demanding to know more of Sarah. Obeying their order, Karen began at Sarah's neck, licking her collarbone as a satisfying moan sang in her ear and long, elegant fingers clung to her back, crushing their bodies together. Sarah's was soft and conformed to Karen's as if they were meant to fit together.

Karen's hands felt the curve of Sarah's breast and cupped the soft mounds. What was it that she'd told Ashton? It wasn't fair that some women got perfect breasts. Sarah's were somewhere between a B and C, not too big, not too small, and fit so nicely in her palms. The soft, sensitive flesh hardened to a tip as her fingers circled, followed by her mouth. Another lyrical moan filled Karen with pride as one hand kneaded Sarah's left breast and her tongue flicked at the hardened nipple that went from a pale pink to flushed and glistening red.

"Jesus," Sarah said as her hand slid down the front of her shorts. Karen felt the rhythm against her stomach that Sarah created. She wanted to feel Sarah everywhere. Taste her as she came. She wanted to be the one who made her cum, not just be the one assisting in her orgasm.

"I can do that for you," Karen offered, and Sarah stilled.

"No." Sarah licked her top lip, pulled it in, then released. "I...oh fuck...I'm not sure if I'm ready for that."

"What's the difference?"

"One is sex and one is foreplay."

"You're not ready for sex with me?"

Karen didn't mean to sound condescending, but she could see the disconnect instantly from Sarah. Her hand came out of her shorts. Karen caught the fingers with her hand, and then brought them to her mouth. She tasted the beginning of Sarah's arousal as she looked on with wide eyes.

"I don't just sleep with people." Sarah's voice was a rasped whisper.

"Neither do I."

"I haven't been with anyone since Lisa." Now Sarah was trembling.

Karen found her lips, but made sure to stay gentle.

"If you're not ready for more, that's fine, but I wanted you to be satisfied. This wasn't about me. It's about you. You've compromised enough for me and my lifestyle. In bed, I want you to have everything you need."

"And out of bed?"

"I'll do the best I can."

"Then let's just stay in bed," Sarah suggested, as she pulled Karen to her and began to unbutton her cotton top. The feel of her delicate hands gliding over Karen's skin had goose bumps erupting, and the hungry kisses began.

Both stripped bare from the waist up Karen kissed all exposed flesh, but Sarah kept slowing Karen down. Something Karen needed more than she realized. Brushing aside Karen's hair, Sarah kissed her neck from behind. Her lips trailed down Karen's spine and it was as if she knew the pressure point that wrapped around to the front of Karen's body. She'd flick her tongue and suck between her shoulders, then again right at the edge of her waist line. Her hands went from cradling Karen's breasts to teasing her belly with air-like brushes. When she'd worked her way back up to Karen's ear she said something unexpected.

"What is it about you? I need to fuck you."

"Was licking me supposed to suppress that?"

"It has in the past."

"That's just mean."

"Why?"

"Because there is no way the woman you did that to didn't want to turn you around and do naughty things to you."

"What kind of naughty things are you talking about?" Sarah's eyes were hooded as Karen could no longer control herself.

Their lips met and Karen laid her back, covering Sarah's with her own. With fevered fingers, they each worked on the other's pants.

"Me first," Karen ordered, and pulled off Sarah's shorts. "I don't know how those other girls didn't tie you down and take you, but I'm gonna make you cry my name."

"A challenge, I like those."

Karen kissed Sarah's lips, then chin, then in between her breasts as she continued to her belly button and, finally, the thin line of trimmed blonde hair. One hundred percent real. Maybe she should stop. Is that why the others did? The words love and forever spun in her head the second she kissed the bright pink lips between Sarah's thighs, and then licked. She was done. Sarah's hips adjusted and Karen's mouth fully took in the swollen nub of Sarah's clit. She suckled it as if she were starving, and wasn't that the truth? She was starving for the love that felt right. The connection she only achieved with women.

Her own core clenched as the flavor, sweet to begin with, became salted. With two fingers at first, she pressed inside Sarah, curving upward in search of the small bundle of nerves. She knew instantly when she hit it from the small clench and deep groan. With a steady rhythm, she lapped Sarah while adding a third finger. The climax came too quickly for her, but she needed to read the signals better to know how to make it last longer. The tease, the build-up of tightening walls until they began to ripple against her fingers.

Then again, there was no reason for her to stop. A climax didn't need to stop her from giving pleasure. Adding a fourth finger, she sucked harder on Sarah's clit, but she tried to pull away. Oh, no, Karen had a goal, and until Sarah was screaming her name, she'd not reached it. Her free arm wrapped around Sarah's waist and she held her face tightly against Sarah's pussy. There was no stopping her. She wanted the scream. She wanted to give Sarah pleasure. Most of all, she wanted Sarah.

* * * *

Sarah's head balanced on its crown as waves of electricity tore through every molecule.

"Holy shit," Sarah screamed.

Sarah's mind was empty of all thought except Karen. She'd dug her way into more than her pants. The worst part was, Mandy was right. Damn. Sarah wanted to be able to separate. She wanted to have an orgasm or four then dump Karen, but that wasn't who she was. Sarah knew what would happen if she didn't stop Karen now. Love. Fucking horrifying and terrible love.

The first orgasm had taken a few minutes, the second and third thundered quickly, clenching her belly in the most sweet and painful way. It needed to stop. She couldn't take any more. Her back was arched and she swore she heard her sheet tear when her nails dug into the fabric.

She couldn't help herself from thrusting her hips against Karen's fingers. They curled upward slightly, so each stroke touched her g-spot. The tiny bundle of nerves that guaranteed success in any sexual endeavor. She'd lost track of how many fingers were inside her, but by the pressure inside her core she assumed it was at least three, if not four. Every inch was being touched and stretched to the point that she understood the thickness factor.

Biting her bottom lip, she tried to keep her pussy planted on Karen's lips, but the urge to stop the sensation before she went over the edge had Sarah fighting with herself. The speed of Karen's fingers caused a friction Sarah thought she'd never recover from. Her core tightened around Karen's perfectly manicured fingers so hard she wasn't sure Karen would be able to pull back, but pull back she did and, with one hard thrust, filled Sarah to the brink.

"Jesus, Karen, no more," Sarah panted. "No…oh fuck."

Still Karen wouldn't relent. When Karen swirled her tongue around Sarah's clit, she was truly done. The fourth orgasm hit and shot up her spine. Every sound in the room became clear. Karen's panting, then a light wind as she blew on Sarah's pussy, sending a shiver down her legs.

Karen kissed the inside of Sarah's thighs up to her knees and back again. She took one long lick from pussy to belly button and back down to kiss down the other leg. It was as if Karen couldn't get enough of Sarah, and as much as the intelligent part of her brain knew she should stop, it was too late. She'd not tripped and fallen down a rabbit hole, she jumped in head first and that little bunny was making it impossible for her to come to grips with reality. Reality that included hiding from the world.

Right now, all Sarah could concentrate on was the way Karen's fingers felt holding her, how her nails trailed down her skin and made it erupt with all sorts of ideas. Ones that kept her touching Sarah at all costs.

Sarah's body crashed back to the bed when Karen released her grip on Sarah's waist. Her body writhed as her hands absently searched for something. Finding what she wanted she practically hauled up Karen into her arms. She clung to Karen as if her life depended upon the feel of her body.

"Don't go," she pleaded. "Please. I need you here."

Their lips fused and Sarah refused to separate. Her right leg latched around Karen's hip, and if it wasn't for Karen still wearing a pair of khaki shorts, they would be one. She hadn't fallen for Karen—fallen would indicate a possible accident. A trip into a pool of love caused by an errant stick on the pathway. No, she'd allowed this to happen, and as she tried to fight every hormone with the sane part of her brain, it was all for naught. Mandy's warnings had echoed off Sarah's thick skull. She couldn't do the quickie sex romp with a hottie. Everything was romance to Sarah and now her vision clouded and ignored the realities of who she was with.

All Sarah could focus on was the rush she felt crashing against her body. The smell of Karen's sweet perfume and the feel of her skin. Her belly was smooth and Sarah ached to taste her in the most personal of ways. She was blind to the bright signs saying *Stay Away. Danger.* And most importantly *Heartbreak Ahead.*

* * * *

What had she done? Karen thought she knew better than to have someone fall in love with her. More importantly, she knew better than to fall in love with a woman. Sure, Ashton could mark her as his for life, but not Sarah. No matter how right it felt being held in her arms. Sarah broke the kiss and fell into the nook of Karen's neck. Curled tightly, she reached for the edge of the comforter and wrapped it around the two of them.

"You shouldn't have done that," Sarah whispered softly.

"I was getting a little cold." Karen giggled.

"Not the blanket."

"I couldn't help myself."

"You need to come out. The repression has you rushing when you get a chance."

"You didn't like that?"

"What you did…" Sarah brushed her thumb across Karen's lower lip. "That I liked a little too much."

"What's the problem exactly?"

Sarah uncurled from the embrace and scooted up in the bed, leaving Karen cold and wanting the warmth to return as she rested her arms and head on Sarah's lap.

"Mandy told me not to date you."

"Why? Because I'll treat you poorly?"

"Nope, because I fall in love too easily. In her words 'I expect people to be there in the morning'."

"And I can't stay past ten."

"You'll break my heart if we stay together." Sarah's cool blue eyes became downturned.

"I don't want to."

"Nobody wants to, but I've been trying to reconcile myself with the thought of seeing you on the side. It feels dirty to me and at the same time I want to see you. And now those stupid hormones are circling my system."

Karen tried to balance out what Sarah was saying. She wasn't asking for anything but a chance at a real relationship. When it came down to it, Karen wanted that, too. A real person to hold her and be by her side always. Sarah wasn't going to settle for less and for the first time, neither was Karen. Now to convince Sarah. Fortunately, Karen had been praised for her ability to calm down and bring together opposition. This just needed a bit of the old Schroeder diplomacy.

"My campaign manager asked if I wanted you on staff."

"Really, like the man candy out there?" Sarah hitched her thumb to the living room.

"It'd let you be close without raising suspicion."

Sarah's eyebrows knitted together and she looked at her hands.

"I told him no." Sarah's head shot up. "Not for the obvious reasons."

"Paying your staff for sex."

"Yeah." Karen lay back on the pillow and let out a long breath of air. "I knew I wouldn't be able to keep my hands off you."

"Unlike previous girlfriends?"

"Fishing?"

"A little," Sarah confessed. "You've had them before. I was just wondering how you dealt with them."

"You're not the only one feeling something different." Karen closed her eyes for a moment, and then let out a small giggle. "I mean, we both chose each other over mini donuts."

"God, it could be love. How the hell did we both let this happen?"

"I don't know, you wanna go to a camp so we can both be cured?"

"There's no cure for you," Sarah confessed and leaned in for another kiss. "If we're going to do this, you'll need to teach me the rules."

"You've already broken most of them…well, more fractured them."

"My friends."

"Yes, that's a big no-no."

"One of them lives with me."

"Dear Lord. Well, I need to meet with all of them and Howard. Can you arrange that?"

"New rule. We're in the bedroom. No talk of hiding out…at least, in the real world."

"Then whatever shall we do?" Karen asked and raised her eyebrow.

"Oh," Sarah said and tucked back an errant strand of hair. "I've got a few dozen ideas."

Chapter Five

"All my life, my heart has yearned for a thing I cannot name."
—Andre Breton

Sarah and Mary Beth stood in the gym for their school as Eli tried to get the foreman, his cousin Raphael, to give a realistic update on overhaul. With a new roof finally in place, they were tearing down the ceiling and fixing the water damage there and on the floor. The men's conversation escalated to Spanish, fast Spanish, leaving the women behind to sit there like idiots.

"Damn, he's hot when he gets like this," Mary Beth said as she nibbled on her bottom lip.

"Do you often have him yell in Spanish at you?"

"He's not yelling at me, he's defending me." Mary Beth's eyes sparkled when she turned to Sarah with a sigh. "He's so getting some tonight."

Mary Beth crossed her arms as her eyebrows knitted together. After dating Eli for nine months, she'd begun to pick up the language. Sarah hoped she knew what was going on because everything suddenly stopped and they'd been summoned to the gym. Not the place she wanted to be at one o'clock in July, especially since the central air hadn't been fixed in this area of the school.

Eli's right hand thrust upward toward the yellowed tiles of the ceiling and the men on the scaffold who had stopped working.

"Tres," he barked.

"I got that one, he said three." Sarah sighed, and then leaned against the wall.

"You're a genius," Mary Beth replied as she rolled her eyes. "Three what? Days? Thousand dollars? Monkeys picking their asses? That's it…" Mary Beth stormed over to Eli. "Pico de gallo."

Both men turned to see the crazy white lady yelling at them. Sarah had to admit it was funny. Mary Beth had been growing out her hair, and it was in the awkward stage before she could pull it out of her eyes so she'd had her hand running through it in frustration.

"Isn't that a sauce?" Sarah asked.

"It's short hand for slow down on the Española for the white chick."

"No, I'm sure it's a food."

Mary Beth turned, crossed her arms, and gave the glare that is dispensed at the hospital once you've given birth. The mom's-going-to-kill-you if you don't stop glare.

"Yes, it's a food, but it's my way of saying stop."

Sarah ducked her head and waited for the verdict. After ten minutes, the men went back to working after what Sarah was sure was someone saying Mary Beth was crazy, but then again, Sarah's Spanish rarely went further than a Taco Bell menu.

"They're going to work through the night for the next three days to get this gutted and flooring put in. It's going to take at least a week after the floor's been treated for us to come back in here and finish."

"What was the hassle?"

"They said they couldn't do the ceiling and walls before the floor was done," Eli said while shaking his head. "I apologize for the lie. It's not that hard to do. I love them, but because I'm family and young they think they can walk all over me. Truthfully they can, just not Mi Reina."

Eli gave Mary Beth a light peck on the lips, and then headed back to the bank where he worked.

"Still his Queen, I see," Sarah teased. That was the one Spanish phrase they all learned.

"Of course, and thank goodness."

They walked back to the far side of the school they'd moved into in June. It would be the daycare center, and it was giving the loyal parents the care they'd come to expect. The four of them had turned a business that was losing money into a profitable care center for children. It was to the point at least twice a year that they had to hire another person because their waiting list had gotten so long.

Mary Beth headed to her office and Sarah decided it was a great time to bring up Karen's proposal.

"Can we talk?" she asked as they reached the doorway. Mary Beth turned around in surprise.

"I thought you headed back to your room."

"Jasmine and Paula are there, I'm fine for a few minutes."

"Sit down."

Mary Beth was still unpacking boxes because it seemed as if every time she had a minute another building issue came up. She moved a pile of files off of one of her chairs and moved it to the other chair that already contained a pile.

"What's up?" she asked, as she rolled into her chair behind her desk.

"You remember Karen?"

"Karen?" Mary Beth's eyebrows came together and her face twisted. "The Representative."

"Oh, lunch lady. With the grants? Did she come up with anything?"

"Not about the school."

"Is this about you giving me the eye?"

"Yes…" Sarah drew out the word.

"And the secret you didn't know was or wasn't a secret?"

"It's a secret."

"Okay, so what's to talk about?"

"Um, she needs to meet with all of us and her campaign manager."

"Why?" Mary Beth scoffed.

"To make sure no one finds out she's family."

"In the family of women, I assume."

"Men are family too, they just don't like women when they are."

"Right." Mary Beth leaned her forearms on her desk and stared at Sarah. Her hazel eyes, with their emerald speckles, were laughing, even though her face appeared serious. "Again, why do I need to meet with this woman?"

"We're dating."

"I got that and yes I'd love to meet the woman you're seeing, but it's not like you're serious. You just met."

55

"Eli had a discussion about coffee and you started checking for a ring immediately."

"He has a deep love for the bean."

"Which one?" Sarah asked with an arched eyebrow.

Mary Beth blushed bright red, coughed, and then sat back.

"We had sex."

"I'm going to see if I can find you and Mandy separate apartments."

"Stop it."

"You just met Karen."

"And…I really like her."

"Obviously."

"I need your help with the others, especially Mandy."

"Sarah," Mary Beth sighed and eyed her best friend. "I don't mind keeping secrets, but it's not healthy. Take it from someone who knows. It eats away at you."

Mary Beth had spent years being her son's father's other woman. Their relationship started like any other until she got pregnant and he ran, but he'd come back to Mary Beth every chance he could even after he got married. It'd been years of Mary Beth coming to work exhausted, not from lack of sleep, but guilt. Since she met Elias, she'd been happy and bubbly. Emotions all the girls had thought disappeared with pregnancy.

"Just let me have a little bit of time with her to see if it goes anywhere. I'm sure if we get serious—"

Mary Beth shot her hand up. "Don't start down that road. If you're going back in the closet that's your choice, but don't put any expectations on Karen. For your sake, not hers. She'll never love you like that."

"You're wrong."

"If I am I'll gladly spend a whole day teaching you to pitch."

"Wow, you're serious about this." Despite all of them being accomplished softball players, and Sarah really wanting to learn how to pitch, she'd never lasted more than a half hour once she started. "What if I break up with her first?"

"Then we'll go the normal thirty minutes when you have me at my wit's end."

"I'm breaking the record."

"Just don't break a window again."

Sarah bit back a retort. "How is your mom doing?" Mary Beth had recently reunited with the mother who had disowned her since Luke was in utero.

"Why did I want to be around my family again? I forgot what it was like to be the oldest of five. Every day it's another thing I'm supposed to attend or visit. At least mom's chemo is done."

"And your dad?"

"Still living the dream I guess. Both their lawyers are telling them not to leave the house so he's lucky there's only two of us left or he wouldn't have a bedroom. I go over and mom and him are acting like it was any other day." Mary Beth shifted papers on her desk and tapped her pen a few times. "How can she forgive him?"

"It's not like they haven't been playing that game for years."

"I don't think they're actually going to get divorced."

"Ariel does." Mandy's mother Ariel, who had been Mary Beth's father's mistress for…well, three months after Mary Beth was conceived. "She was over a week ago with wedding magazines. Mandy had this blank stare the whole time."

"We've perfected that look. Especially when Dad just wants time with his two girls."

Sarah had to laugh at that one. Kevin Wallace had to be the most self-centered man in the world, yet at the same time, he put out the image of a devoted family man who puts everyone's needs before his own. A master manipulator. If Mary Beth would have learned about Mandy in high school her whole world would have been destroyed, but after years of being in the real world, Sarah knew she just saw him as one of many. The rose colored glasses of her youth fell to the wayside when she'd been kicked out for making probably the only mistake in her whole life.

"So Gwen and Jilly Bean aren't his girls?"

"He's delusional on all things family. They don't know Mandy's their sister."

"On that note, I better get back to the classroom."

"It's not a classroom," Mary Beth reminded Sarah. "It's a structured learning environment. Our classrooms aren't open until the day after

Labor Day."

"You and Gabbie need to get out more."

"Is someone offering babysitting services?"

"For demon spawn and the next Mafia members?"

"Yes."

"Maybe, after you all meet with my girlfriend."

Just saying girlfriend made it feel official in Sarah's mind. She wondered if Karen was using the same vernacular.

* * * *

"What has you smiling from ear to ear?" Howard asked as he plopped a takeout bag on Karen's desk.

"I'm happy to be done with the fair."

"Are you ready for this week's schedule?"

"No," Karen sighed.

"You have three fundraising dinners this week," Howard continued without missing a beat. "Ashton's been informed since one is black tie, not just business dress."

"Prom dress?" Karen grumbled and dropped her head on the desk.

"Award show, not prom dress. You're a grown up now."

"That has yet to be proven," Karen said as she began digging into her Styrofoam takeout container. Inside was the famously misspelled Jucy Lucy and fries. "What do you want?"

"To get through your schedule without snotty comments."

"You got me a Jucy Lucy. You never let me have them unless..." A knock at the door led to a press crew coming through the door without asking permission.

"Hello, Representative Schroeder," the first reporter said. "Have you heard there's a big competition between the 5-8 and Nook for the best Jucy Lucy?"

"Yes I have, the top seller today I assume wins?"

"Yes," the reporter grinned. "And we see you're supporting the Nook."

"It's exclusively in my district. Of course I'm supporting them. I love the way they're made. I got addicted in high school."

A Jucy Lucy was a hamburger with a hunk of cheese injected right in the middle of it. When you bit down the cheese oozed, and if it was too close to when the hamburger came off the griddle, you could end up with a second-degree burn. Luckily Capitol Hill was a good ten minute drive from the Nook so she could take a nice, big bite with a thumbs-up for the camera.

"You could have warned me," she growled at Howard when the reporters had left.

"And you could have told me you snuck out with Ashton to get laid last night."

Karen wiped her lips from the greasy burger and steadied herself.

"He's my fiancé, isn't he?"

"He's not who you slept with."

"That's your assumption." Karen leaned back in her chair with her arms crossed.

"I'm trying to be respectful—"

"Try harder," she growled.

"Leave the woman alone until after you're in Washington."

"Because three thousand miles with only traceable texts and instant messages will be easier to hide?"

"You need to focus on the election."

"If you think I lost my focus in one night, I shouldn't be in the race." Karen stood and pointed her index finger down on the desk. "If Ashton and I eloped last night to Vegas you wouldn't say boo, you'd have a damn cake for me by the time I landed."

"That's not the same and you know it." Howard huffed and ran his fingers through his gray hair. "How many sex scandals do you think the party can handle?"

"Is it because it's another woman?"

"Actually it's because you are."

Karen's eyebrows knitted together.

"Men in the party can have affairs," Howard said and took a seat. Karen followed. "Women can't. That's why Ash doesn't worry me. He could put out a sex tape with three men, and as long as you hold his hand while you accept him back after rehab I could get his ass elected."

"She won't be a distraction."

"I know she won't when it comes to events and meetings. I know

59

you'll put the election first, but what I don't know is if she can be hidden."

"Ash bought me a burner cell with cash. I was going to give her that number to use."

"How are you going to spend time with her? Realistically. That's explainable."

"Can't we get an apartment in her building for a staff member?"

"Ash is the only staff member we can trust and last I knew he owns his condo."

"Fuck."

"Talk with her, ask her to wait until after November."

"That's five months away."

"If she likes you as a person—"

"Don't make me come around this desk. She's not like the others. I'm setting up a meeting with her friends so you can explain the rules."

Howard let out a long breath and steepled his fingers.

"She's told people already?" he growled.

"She has a roommate and partners at her job…"

"That's why you let me vet people!" Howard stood and tossed his arms up in the air.

"Calm down."

"Why? You're throwing everything away."

"Eventually I was going to be out."

"After your second term in the Senate, I hoped."

"What? When I'm fifty? Sixty? That doesn't happen overnight. I want a family. I want a life."

"No, you never wanted that. If you did, you'd fuck men like you're supposed to."

His words slapped her harder than any hand ever could. Howard had never made her feel bad about her preference.

"This is who I am," she croaked, trying to hold back the tears. "You understood that. When you asked me to run eight years ago, you were the second person I told in the world. Do you know how scary that was for me? Gut wrenching?" Karen placed her hand on her chest in hopes the pain would go away. "Do you understand the trust I put in you? You said it wouldn't be a problem. You said I could be whatever I wanted

60

and you'd help me achieve my dreams no matter what."

"I thought you'd get past it. You were twenty-two and fresh out of college. You didn't know what you wanted."

"I told you when I was six I wanted to be President. I'm not the type of person to change my mind when I make a choice. You were the only one who kept that dream alive for me. Snapping me back in place when I screwed up at school, telling me the classes to take and clubs to join."

"I guess I should have told you which boys to date."

"You need to leave. You need to leave now."

"Karen, you kick me out now, you're done at the end of your term."

"The Republican Party asked for me."

"No, they asked for the person they think you are. Nobody wants you."

Howard left the office and Ashton came through the door and closed it behind him.

"Cancel my meetings today."

"We have a fundraiser tonight."

"Then I'll go, but this afternoon I need to be alone."

"What happened?"

"Get. Out." Karen growled.

"Kare Bear," Ashton said with a slight lilt to his voice.

"I will rip out your heart and eat it."

"Then I suppose you could skip the dinner, but people might talk."

Karen hated when Ashton used his calm voice. She wanted to be mad. She wanted to be hurt. She wanted to hurt somebody. Worse yet she wanted to be in Sarah's arms hiding in the bedroom. There she could be herself.

Defeated, she laid her head on her desk.

"What's the word, hummingbird?"

Karen breathed out, took in a deep, cleansing breath, and lifted her head so she was resting comfortably on her folded hands.

"You still have that list of campaign managers?"

"Yes," Ashton said, then sat in the chair across from her and leaned his forearms on his thighs. "Why are we firing Howard?"

"I think he quit."

"You think?"

61

"It sounded that way, but then…" Karen let out a gust of air. "Do you believe being gay is a choice?"

Ashton's blue eyes looked up with sincerity. "No, maybe when I was younger, but I can see how painful it is for you to not be yourself. No one would choose that. Most days you walk around like you're wearing wool underwear. Is Howard pissed about last night?"

"Among other things. I just met Sarah, but I could really see settling down with her."

"You're not a settling type person."

"Settling for? No, settling down, having roots, a family. Oh look who I'm talking to."

"I'd take offense if it wasn't true." Ashton's patented ruler-of-his-domain smile crossed his lips and stretched out. "I love not being tied down, with the exception of a good set of handcuffs."

"Slut, we're talking about me right now." Karen spun her index finger around to bring him out of his world of bondage and strategic spanking.

"Will you both be wearing dresses or is she more butch than I thought?"

"Howard says I can't be in public office and have sex with women."

"Why not? It never stopped, Roosevelt, Kennedy, or Clinton."

"I guess I'm in the wrong party."

"Why is that again?"

"Too rich to know better."

"Oh yeah…that's it. The stuck-ups in the party are dying off."

"And being replaced by idiots."

"Why don't you just become an independent? Socially you're a Dem, fiscally you're a Rep."

"Being a lesbian doesn't make me a Democrat."

"You voted for that school lunch program."

"Did you see the other five bills attached to that one?"

"I'm window dressing, I don't read." Ashton gave her a little wink.

"Exactly. I don't know what else to be." Karen began doodling on a scrap piece of paper. "Would I have to be a lawyer?"

"Oh, now we're talking about jobs. I thought you were going to veer off into some weird place." He sighed and looked at his hands. "Howard isn't who determines your future. The voters are. The only reason I could see them not voting for you is me."

"Why you?"

"Because you lied. I know Howard thinks it's best to have the man candy, but it would have been better if it was just speculated we were together."

"I thought you didn't think?"

"I don't. I'm not a fool and neither are you." Ashton's lips pursed, then let out a gust of air. "The party is opening up like the rest of the world. But...sex scandals involve a man lying to his wife." Ash folded his hands in front of him. "You lied to the voters, that's where they get pissed, and that's what you're going to have to get forgiveness for."

Chapter Six

"The greatest sign of success for a teacher is to be able to say, "The children are now working as if I did not exist."
—*Maria Montessori*

"That's very good Max and Luke," Sarah said as she checked their bead chain where they'd counted to five hundred and fifty. "Are you done or will you be working more this afternoon?"

"I want a snack," Max said. "Then Luke and I will be goin' to a thousand."

"A thousand, that's a lot of work. You better get a snack to keep your energy up."

Sarah smiled and pulled out her assessment book to add the boys' progress. Even though she was in the day care section of Growing Strong, soon enough she'd have her first classroom and she couldn't be more excited. Getting off the small stool she used to observe, she moved to an area where she could watch Trudy and Zack, who were working on a puzzle of Africa.

Max and Luke had each taken a few crackers and pre-sliced cheese for a snack. They were at the small table with two chairs set aside in the snack area. Each of them had laid out their placemats and poured themselves a glass of water. It amazed her the way the kids could handle every day activities with such ease, especially when she had visited a traditional school where the kids had problems with even sitting still. There is something about the Montessori method that cultivated a peaceful environment. Sure, they'd occasionally have an outburst or case of the wild child, but overall her room was controlled.

"No, that's South Africa, 'member, Ms. Sarah said it looks like a peanut," Trudy said to Zack.

"Oh, yeah, at the bottom," Zack said and placed the puzzle piece.

"Sarah," Jasmine interrupted Sarah's train of thought. "You have a visitor."

Sarah's eyebrows knitted together and she turned to see Karen in the doorway. Sarah smiled at the sight of Karen in an olive colored business suit. She looked so uptight, but professional, compared to Sarah in her polo and khakis. Karen's hair was perfectly styled and framed her face, but there was something there that worried Sarah.

"I didn't expect to see you here," she said as she approached Karen.

"I wanted to see your school."

Her voice was sincere, but her eyes told the truth. Something was wrong, very wrong.

"This is a day care room, let me take you to the construction zone." Sarah turned to Jasmine. "You're good for a few minutes?" she nodded, and Sarah and Karen went into the hall.

"Will I need a hard hat?" Karen asked.

"Not with that hair," Sarah teased. "It looks like it's pretty solid."

"Way to break a girl's heart." They walked up the hallway to the school annex. "Don't you know you never comment on a woman's hair?"

"It's perfect, but I liked it better last night. You teased it a little too much today."

"I have a fundraiser tonight and had to meet with a few people up at the State House for committee work earlier today."

"Don't forget your burger choice. You might have alienated half your voters with that one."

"It wasn't my choice. How'd you hear about that?"

"I follow you on *Twitter*."

"Oooh…is that a new thing?"

"Very. I figured it'd be an easy way to keep up with you, I'm just one of many so…"

"Stop," Karen said, then looked up and down the hallway. "I want to be with you. I'm not coming out, I can't right now, but I won't be hiding who I am for long, I promise. Something came up today and…" Karen brushed back a few strands of Sarah's hair and stepped into her personal space. Sarah's breath hitched. "All I could think about was you. Please tell me I'm not the only one wanting more."

"You're not," Sarah said, her voice barely above a whisper.

"Good. My life is a whirlwind during elections. Every step I take, every…" she shook her head.

"Move you make…they're watching you."

The two women smiled at one another.

"Something like that." Karen chuckled. "November, after I'm elected, I'll be ready… not before. I need to know you can handle that."

A lumped formed in Sarah's chest. It was only a few months away. They were over halfway through July. Karen was giving her a deadline, a time when she would be in a safe place.

Sarah's hands twined with Karen's and she pulled them behind her back so Karen's arms were wrapped around her. Their bodies pressed against each other and Sarah leaned in for a kiss. Slow, deep, and lingering. Their tongues touched briefly and the moan from Karen vibrated against Sarah's lips.

Breathless, Karen pulled back.

"Ugh, don't do that to me," she growled.

"No kissing."

"Yes, in public."

"There's no one here," Sarah replied innocently.

"But someone could come through the door."

"Then let go of my hands and put some space between us."

"I *really* don't want to do that," Karen purred.

Sarah's lips curled up and she tried to not be too obvious in her excitement.

"Does this mean I have to be the grownup?"

"Please, you're the one thing I don't want planned or controlled."

"Except when it comes to who knows what."

"Right, don't hate me."

"Impossible."

"This can work, right?"

"If you want it to. I'm willing to gamble on love one more time, but to warn you, those girls that are trying to not be seen as peepers behind you will kill you if you break my heart."

Karen's fingers released Sarah's and she turned sharply on her heel to see Gabbie, Mary Beth, and Mandy at the end of the hallway with scowls on their faces.

* * * *

"Oh shit," Karen said under her breath. "How long have they been there?"

"Not long," Mary Beth said. "We heard we needed to talk to you about something."

Karen cleared her throat and tried to compose herself. "I was just telling Sarah I need to keep our relationship under wraps for a few months."

The girls kept those scowls on their faces and their arms crossed. Not the worst audience Karen had ever faced, but her knotted stomach was her private acknowledgement of her nerves.

"Why?" the dark haired woman who had to be Gabbie asked.

"I'm not out."

"We don't really understand that," Mandy said. "More like we worry there's shame involved that centers around Sarah and that pisses us off."

"No," Karen assured them as she stepped closer. "Sarah's amazing, but we are new and I could lose everything."

"How long?" Mandy asked. "A few weeks? Months? Years? And so you know, that's a loaded question."

"Right." Karen nervously licked her lips and let her hand fall back in search of Sarah, who thankfully took it. "I told Sarah after the election."

"Can we get that in writing?" Gabbie asked.

"In writing?" Karen laughed. "You don't…" the look on the three women's faces let her know they were serious, dead serious.

"You don't need—" Sarah began.

"No," Mandy cut her off. "You're thinking with your girly parts, we're your brain right now."

"I am not," Sarah said indignantly.

"There's no air conditioning in this part of the school," Mandy said with a droll annoyance as she raised her right eyebrow.

Karen turned to see Sarah's face flushed red and her arms crossed in front of her chest.

"Yep, so, as we were saying…" Mandy continued.

"No," Sarah interjected again. "If she breaks her word it's on me to handle it."

"Fine, but if she breaks your heart it's on us," Gabbie said.

"Like you did so much to Lisa."

The girls all looked at each other daring the other to spill. Mandy, who Karen was starting to notice was the muscle of the group, finally fessed up.

"It was really convenient of her to never call or try to get back with you, isn't it?"

"What did you do?" Sarah balked.

"It's better for all parties involved that you not be able to incriminate any of us," Mary Beth said, then picked up some trash on the floor and tossed it into a nearby bin.

The love Sarah's friends had for her made Karen feel safe for some reason. They wouldn't tell on her because it would hurt Sarah. Strangely, for the first time, Karen felt comfortable to be herself in their company, and she put her arm around Sarah's waist.

"I promise I won't hurt her."

"Oh, that's just protecting yourself, not her," Mandy warned with a growl, then strangely smiled. "In our group we only talk sex and relationships with each other, not outsiders."

"Thank you," Karen said with slight hesitation from uncertainty.

"You want a real tour?" Sarah asked. "Or do you have somewhere to be?"

"I have to get ready for a fundraiser and locate a new campaign manager."

"How did you lose a campaign manager before the primary?" Sarah asked.

"Long story. He might still be around and just need a cooling off period." Karen slipped her hand down and let if fall into Sarah's. "I'll be out late with Ash tonight, but I think I have time on Wednesday if you're interested."

"Wednesday we have softball," Gabbie interjected. "Sorry, I didn't mean to butt in."

"Yes you did," Sarah smiled. "We've got a killer softball team. I suppose there is no way you could watch us play."

"None I could think of off the top of my head, but if you don't mind a late night visitor tomorrow night, I'm done with meetings by nine-thirty."

"I could work with that."

"I'm sure *you* could," Mandy sniped. "I have a Trailer Park Makeover marathon."

"We'll keep the door closed," Sarah assured.

"You bringing the grunting animal?" Mandy asked Karen.

"Animal? Oh...Ash...yeah, we're kind of a package deal." Karen crossed her arms. "When did you and Ash talk?"

"I came home last night. He's a deep thinker there. He wouldn't let me watch Bride Battle."

"That was on last night?" Mary Beth chimed in.

"The reunion show." Mandy gave Karen a death glare that let her know she'd have to have a discussion with Ashton.

"Why didn't he let you watch it?" Karen queried.

"Something about a politician on local access. It was boring. Not even one hair pull or shoes being used as weapons."

"That's not strange," Karen said with all seriousness. "There are more men in politics, so it's all about throwing folding chairs for distance, but you have to avoid voters. It's extremely hard to do competitively."

"Is that how you won your district?" Mandy asked.

"Test me." Karen may have only had a few years on the State Floor, but she understood the need to show strength to the pride.

"She'll work." Mandy tapped the other girl's shoulders and they left.

"Wow," Sarah exclaimed. "No one's passed the test that quickly."

Karen turned and pulled Sarah into her arms. Sarah reciprocated, only her hands landed on Karen's hips and ass. A shiver took off through Karen's body as she stared into Sarah's blue eyes. Her lips found Sarah's, but not in a claiming way. She wanted to brush the delicate skin against hers.

"I only took the test because it was important to you. I've noticed

69

how close you are with your friends."

Sarah rewarded Karen's efforts with a deeper kiss. One that had so much meaning to it she was unsure of how to react. Her lips tingled and her body trembled. Sarah pulled away and pushed Karen. The sudden break felt as if someone had physically ripped them apart.

"Grownup…if I don't stop I'm going to have a lot of explaining to do."

"Right," Karen agreed, only to bring her hands forward and cup Sarah's cheeks so they could kiss just once more. "You are irresistible."

Sarah stilled in Karen's arms. She could see her holding back and Karen feared she'd unknowingly said something wrong.

"You better go or you'll be late. Tomorrow night I expect you in my bed."

* * * *

"I have a problem," Sarah said the instant Jasmine and Cara took the kids out for recess.

"That is?" Mandy asked as she stabbed at a melon piece in her bowl with a fork.

"I'm in love."

Mandy didn't look up from her bowl of fruit. Instead she slowly chewed, swallowed, and got another piece of fruit.

"Did you hear me?" Sarah asked. "I said I'm in love."

"Oh yeah, I heard you. Just not gonna comment."

"Since when do you not comment?"

"Since I've had to hold my tongue around Mary Beth's family. I have small moments where I'm free to vent and those are fun, but this isn't one of them."

"Why not?"

"Because small kids aren't allowed to hear cuss words at work."

"Small kids aren't allowed to hear them anywhere," Mary Beth said as she came in the room with a stack of paperwork. "My swear jar runneth over, Auntie Mandy."

"Hey…he was supposed to be sleeping," Mandy retorted.

"He was. Until you and Jillian started a pillow fight."

"I won that, don't let her fool you."

70

"Congrats, you beat up your fifteen-year-old sister."

"I've got years to make up for, and why is it that we can't tell her yet?"

"I don't know."

"Can I?" Sarah offered. "You know, just let it slip? Hey Jilly-Bean, your dad's a slut and set up franchises all over town."

"Maybe...no. No," Mary Beth acquiesced. "Why were you talking about cussing anyway?"

"Sarah's in love."

"That's great," Mary Beth gushed.

"You would say that."

"Hey, I still believe in love."

"That's because you are in love. Wait till ole Eli starts setting up franchises all over town."

"Eli's not like that."

"Yeah, you and Gabbie got the good ones," Mandy sighed.

"You'll find someone, too," Sarah said, but could instantly hear the pity in her voice. "I didn't mean that the way it sounded."

"I never said I was looking. That's for you guys. I'm all about serial-one-night-monogamy...for the most part."

"Is she saying what I think she is?" Mary Beth balked.

"Yes, more than one person has left her room in the morning. She's very French sometimes."

"You let her bring them to your home?"

"I pay half the rent," Mandy snapped. "If I'm really lucky, she'll make them breakfast."

"That only happened once, by accident."

"Right," Mandy teased, then held up air quotes. "By accident. You know you needed that guy's—"

The bustle of kids in the hallway had the teachers scrambling to finish their afternoon snack and ready the room for the final hours of class.

"I need you guys to look over the final order for your classrooms before I place the order."

"Yes, ma'am," Sarah said as Luke came running full speed at Mary Beth and wrapped his arms around her legs.

"Mama," he squealed. "I'm making cookies this afternoon. Will you come back and eat some with me?"

"I could fit that into my schedule. Now remember Luke, no running in the classrooms."

"Yes, Mama." He took off, then stopped and walked to meet Max.

* * * *

"Ready?" Sarah asked Mandy after she'd closed down her room.

"Yep." Mandy still had four kids in her room, but Gabbie was on closing duties. "I'm thinking of adding a few more abacuses to my order. How many will be in your room?"

"Four," Sarah replied as she opened her car door, got in, then buckled. The second her seatbelt clicked she was attacked.

"Are you fucking kidding me?" Mandy screeched inside the car, causing Sarah to jump. "A mother fucking closeted woman. One who lives in the fucking public eye and has no goddamn intention of coming out because it'll ruin her life. Sarah, Jesus fucking Christ, orgasm does not equal love. How many times do I need to say this until you get it through your fucking brain? Oh. My. God. I told you to have a one-night-stand before you tried for a relationship so you could learn the difference, but no, you had to fuck some woman who doesn't even love herself so she could never love you."

Sarah felt as if Mandy had whipped her about the head with a pistol. Hell, she knew words could hurt, but between the content of the words, the violence in which Mandy said them, and the fact that Mandy had held in her frustration for three hours left Sarah gripping the steering wheel for support as she stared straight ahead.

"Tell me how you really feel? I hate when you try to spare my feelings."

''Nope, I'm done."

"You sure? Because there has to be something else you want to say."

"Dumb," Mandy flipped up one of her fingers, then the second. "Closeted, orgasm, romance, love." Her hand was open wide. "I think that covers it…unless…nope, I'm done. No reason to beat a dead horse."

Sarah turned the engine over and pulled away from the center.

"What does it feel like?" Mandy asked as they crossed under Interstate Ninety Four.

"I thought you knew all the physical sensations."

"Love, how does it feel? You just met Karen and you're already declaring your love for her."

Sarah didn't know how to describe the rush she felt when Karen was around. It was different than when she was with Lisa. Lisa took time getting to know her, but with Karen it was instantaneous. Her body flushed and tingled when she looked into Karen's eyes. Smelling her shampoo when she held her close sent her to another place. But she knew Mandy, and she'd need facts and analogies.

"Have you ever had more than a physical response to anyone?"

"Like what?"

"Like your brain feels light because she's around."

"Your brain? Seriously? That sounds like she's drugging you."

"I am jonesing for her right now."

Chapter Seven

"Whenever you find yourself on the side of the majority, it is time to pause and reflect."

—*Mark Twain*

Karen sat in the passenger seat of Ashton's car with her eyes closed. Crossing her legs at the ankles, she let the air conditioning cool her down. It would be so simple with Ashton. He knew how she was and when she needed space or a push. Right now, she was trying to get her brain to settle down. A million scenarios were running through her mind, but she needed to try to grab the most important one, cling to it, and get it resolved.

"We're about five minutes out," Ashton said softly.

"Who are these people?"

"Officially or unofficially?"

"Officially, The Open Heart Society."

"Unofficially?"

"The Tea Party...light."

"Light?"

"Philanthropy more for the tax deduction than the desire to unite the world."

"Hmm...does anyone ever do things for the good of others and not themselves?"

Ashton laughed and Karen opened her eyes to see the lake on the side of the interstate with the sun setting behind it.

"Did you set up interviews for tomorrow?" Karen asked as she kept her gaze out the window.

"You were serious about that?"

"Howard seemed as determined to quit as I did to stay with Sarah. I guess I'm the same way. I want what I want and I'm tired of compromising."

"You've compromised enough."

Karen turned and looked in Ashton's sweet eyes before he turned back to the road ahead and exited the highway.

"I'll make the phone calls after the dinner."

"Thank you."

"Don't thank me…I'm trying to get away from your speech."

When they arrived, Karen straightened out her red business suit and made sure all her buttons were buttoned before she threw on her smile and entered the building.

"Representative Schroeder, thank you so much for attending tonight," a short, stocky man with a large belly said as he vigorously shook her hand. The tight, wet grip of the nervous constituent was draining her resolve.

"Dick Martin," Ashton whispered in her ear.

"Thank you for having me, Mr. Martin," she replied, trying to retrieve her hand without hurting his feelings.

"Oh, call me Dick," he replied and led her into the convention room at the local hotel.

She hadn't even noticed the name the hotels were blurring together. Accordion dividers pressed up against the wall because they were using two rooms. There were at least eighty round tables with ten chairs apiece, and in the middle of each, a set of American flags in a centerpiece. By the windows were a set of rectangular tables on an elevated platform with a podium in the middle, and along the wall were another set of tables with desserts and drinks.

Karen waved as she entered the room and was greeted by applause and a standing ovation. She shook hands as she approached the stage, and was then greeted by a woman who eyed her with envy as she looked over Karen's shoulder at Ashton.

"Hello," Karen said as she met the woman and received another light whisper from Ashton. "Doctor Kennard, it is so nice to meet you finally."

"And you, that legislation you pushed through about the vaccines is a Godsend to those who are in the less fortunate areas."

"Thank you."

"Too bad it was attached to that bill about the homosexuals."

The biting sting cut into Karen as her smile got wider.

"The only way to get anything accomplished is to compromise with the other side. I got what I wanted and they got what they did."

Karen wasn't a fan of the vaccine bill due to the level it ended up cutting from other programs, but Dr. Kennard didn't need to know what she'd wanted out of that legislation.

"Excuse me," a familiar voice said as Howard stepped up to Karen and placed his hand on her shoulder. "I need just two minutes with the Representative before we start the festivities."

"Not a problem. The Father isn't here to give the blessing yet anyway."

"I thought you quit," Karen growled when they'd stepped into the hall.

"Have I ever quit on you?" Howard asked as he tucked his hands in his pockets. "I needed to cool off and regroup that's all."

"Well, Ash already has made phone calls to possible campaign managers."

"You really gonna fire your old pal?"

"My personal life—"

"Is none of my business," Howard said, then shifted his weight. "Well it is, but…I have no right to judge your choices, I just need to help keep it private if you intend to win."

Howard rocked back on his heels and gave Karen his patented stare.

"Your goal is to win," Karen replied.

"Always, but I need to know, what is your goal?"

"To be a good person and be happy."

"So, Washington is out of the picture." Howard let out a light laugh.

"I'm stronger than you give me credit for."

"When do you plan to go public?"

"Not here," Karen replied with a shiver. "That's for damn sure."

"Good, you're not a fool."

"Excuse me." A woman interrupted in the hallway. "Representative, the priest is here."

"Wonderful," Karen gushed. "I'm starving."

* * * *

The weeks went by and Sarah became used to the scattered schedule and late night phone calls from Karen. Stolen moments made their time together seem precious, and her need to discover everything about Karen was her daily quest. Although Sarah hated the confinement of her bedroom, she did enjoy the privacy it afforded them. Since leaving Ashton behind in any fashion wasn't an option, and Sarah wasn't about to leave him alone in her room, she and Karen had fallen into a pattern.

They each had phone calls to make in the evening, Karen to various donors and party members, and Sarah to prospective parents. They'd make the calls without skipping a beat. Their fingers stroking the other's arm or playing with hair as if it were an unconscious act neither could control.

"Holy shit!" Sarah exclaimed as she jumped from the bed, reading the text she'd just received and praying it was a mistake.

"Oh hell no," came from the living room as Mandy received the same notification.

By the time Sarah had opened her bedroom door Mandy's hand had already wrapped around the knob and she fell into Sarah's room.

"You see it?" Mandy stupidly asked.

"Of course I did," Sarah replied as Mandy scanned the bedroom.

"This is what you do all night?" Mandy waved her hand over the piles of papers strewn across the bed and Karen sitting dumbfounded with her laptop open. "You come in here and do your homework all night?"

"Not all the time."

"I'm stuck with Magilla Gorilla out there watching CSPAN and you two aren't even swapping orgasms."

"Mandy, what are we going to do about second base."

"Looks like you can't even get to first."

Sarah slapped Mandy upside her head as both their phones went off. Mary Beth was calling Sarah which only meant Gabbie was in panic mode on Mandy's phone.

"We saw," Sarah answered her phone. "Do we have anyone we could move around?"

"No," Mary Beth said, and both phones were put on speaker.

After a few minutes of over exaggerated panic about the game the next night, Karen stood up and loudly said, "They'll call you right back," and took both phones from Sarah and Mandy, who now returned Karen's earlier dumbfounded look.

"If you guys would have shared the problem instead of hyperventilating, I could have offered a solution," Karen said as she put a hand on each of the ladies' shoulders and led them out of the bedroom. "It's a co-ed league, correct?"

"Yes," Sarah replied warily.

"And you're down one player?"

"If you're suggesting what I think you're suggesting…" Mandy warned.

"The gorilla was All-State three years in a row."

"I was what?" Ashton asked from his dazed focus on the latest issues of the day.

"A pretty good ballplayer."

"Don't," Sarah hissed as Mandy prepared for a great retort. "He played baseball, not really the same thing."

It's not that the girls had a prejudice against baseball players, some of their friends were. Hey, Luke's dad, Nate, had been a good ball player. That didn't mean they wanted him anywhere near their team. Then again, they rarely wanted Nate anywhere near them at all either.

"Hear me out," Karen began.

"Ask me first," Ashton snapped.

"Come on Ash, you were an amazing first baseman."

"Oh," Mandy said as she tilted her head to the side with her awe-shucks face. "We have a first baseman."

"I'm sure whoever they are could move," Karen suggested and Sarah dropped her head. "Oh…you're the first base…woman."

"Did she just call me a first basewoman?" Mandy growled.

"It is nicer than what most people call you," Sarah teased.

"The last thing I would want to do would be to take the job from a harpy," Ashton beamed.

"Troglodyte," Mandy returned fire.

"Oh my God," Sarah cooed. "Our kids are using their words."

"Before you know it they might even form full sentences," Karen pointed out.

"And they're using literary references."

"Technically only yours was. I'm sure Ash learned his from a cartoon."

"Since when do you have a problem with Scooby Doo? Either way," Ash sighed. "I'm washing my hair that day."

"You don't even know when it is," Sarah said.

"I have a very strict hair management routine." Ashton ran his fingers through his hair. "Can't take any chances."

"Yes, you will," Karen ordered. "That way I can see my baby play." She wrapped her arm around Sarah's waist and rested her hand on her hip.

"I'll call Mary Beth and let her know we have a second baseman," Sarah said as she turned back to her bedroom.

After calling and calming down the rest of the team with the news that they'd found a replacement player, Sarah crawled up the bed and straddled Karen's hips.

"You took care of me."

"I do what I can for my voters." A seductive smile crossed her lips.

"Is that all I am to you, a voter?" Sarah asked as her arms wrapped around Karen's neck.

"Not by a long shot." Karen pulled Sarah to her as they fell into an embrace that quickly turned into a swapping of orgasms.

* * * *

"All right," Sarah's mother began as she placed a glass of sun tea in front of Sarah. The glass already beaded with condensation from the warm August sun. "What's kept you from us?"

Her mother sat across from her at the old picnic table in her childhood back yard.

"I'm two weeks from opening the school," Sarah began, and then took a long gulp of the cool tea. "And you know our summer league is in full swing."

"It's an adult league, you play two games max a week. You could have stopped by a few times. I haven't seen you since the fair."

"Really?" Sarah asked as if she was sure she'd been by at least once. "I'm sorry."

"I know you kids are all grown...well, most of you, but it'd be nice to see you occasionally."

"Becca's senior year is eating at you, huh?"

"No," her mom scoffed, and then took a drink. Sarah raised an eyebrow at her and her mother caved. "Okay, yes I pushed Jens and you out the door with glee, but it's so quiet around here."

"I always knew Becca was your favorite."

"She is not. I love you all equally."

Becca came in the backyard with her face fixed on her phone. Her sister wore all black and it appeared she'd recently dyed her hair.

"I retract my previous comment. You've lost her." Sarah waved her hand in front of her sister's phone and received a scowl. "Are we going for the Emo look? If so I think you were misinformed on the uniform."

"I died the tips of my hair black, not all of it," she growled. Rebecca had the lightest blonde hair of all the Lindstrom children. Now with the bottom inch dyed jet black. "I'm trying to be an individual, not a number."

"How many other kids have the same dye job?" Sarah chided her sister.

"Look lesbiatron, it's a style thing...that's something your people don't understand."

"The lipstick ones do," Sarah snapped.

Becca's hormones tended to put her in a bad mood for all twenty-eight days of her period. Sadly, Sarah hadn't lucked out and picked one of the four good ones. Damn. Becca didn't care Sarah was a lesbian, but it was the quickest way they could fight. Sarah had started by calling her Emo...the furthest thing from Becca any day. She was all about popularity and setting trends.

"Girls, girls, you're both pretty," their mom interjected before it became a knock down drag out. "Sit down, Becca, and catch up with your sister."

"I'm the captain this year for dance team, my senior pics make me look fat, and mom refuses to let me retake them. My boyfriend has three colleges offering him scholarships." Becca said as she tossed her phone to the side and drank the rest of Sarah's drink. "Can I leave now?"

"Communication goes two ways," their mom grumbled. "See…this is why you need to come by more often for dinner."

"I'll start trailing the pizza delivery guy more often so I know when it is."

Becca choked a little as she crunched a piece of ice from the glass. Now it was the girls against mom stage of the conversation.

"Has she been this needy for long?" Sarah asked Becca.

"Oh, my, God, I can't walk through the house without being pulled into a bear hug. I think she's going through the change."

"That is not true."

"You're not going through the change or you don't accost your children randomly?"

Their mother crossed her arms and gave the death glare to the two of them.

"You still haven't caught us up?" her mom snipped at Sarah.

"School's opening, I'm up to twenty kids in my class. The softball team is over five hundred this season." Sarah reached for the pitcher of sun tea and refilled her glass, then brought it to her lips. "I've met someone." She swallowed quickly hoping they missed the comment.

"Is she a lipstick lesbian?" her sister teased.

"Kinda," Sarah let out a long gust of air. "I'm not really supposed to talk about our relationship because of her job."

"So it's not serious," her mother said.

"It is, I'm in love with her. We've been together for a month now."

"She's the reason you haven't been by."

"Partially, if my free time and hers coincide, then I'll be with her, but we're both very busy. This month I may not see her much."

"How did you meet?"

"At the fair, she had a booth, too."

"What was she selling that makes it so she can't be in the open with you?"

"Herself," Sarah said. A nervous chill ran up her spine. "She's a politician."

"Oh…" her mother took in a deep, worried breath. "What level?"

"Level? Oh, she's running for congress."

"Wow," Becca's excited tone surprised Sarah. "Impressive."

"I don't like liars."

"Not all politicians lie."

"That's why you're a secret."

Sarah tried to tell herself her mother was just being protective, but it was hard to ignore the same nagging feeling she'd been having. If you can't trust a person with the little things, how can you trust them with the big ones?

"She's Republican. If she wants the seat, she has to be what they expect."

"Then why is she a Republican?"

"She agrees with most parts of the party's platform."

"Oh my God," Becca moaned. "She's talking like a news anchor. Can I leave before I puke?"

"Don't you have to binge before you purge?" Sarah teased, only to receive her second sisterly scowl of the day. "I want you to meet her, then you'll see. She's amazing."

"I've been fliered to death over the last three weeks, maybe you could point out which one she is. Let me dig through the recycling later."

"I want you to meet her," Sarah said again as she placed her hand over her mother's. "I really like her and I think this is long term, not BS like Lisa was."

"I liked Lisa," Becca said as she began rubbing her neck. "She could get rid of any of my headaches." She raised an eyebrow at Sarah. "Well…except for you."

"She only did it so we could get you to pass out and we could have wild monkey sex on your bed."

"Do lesbians have anything but wild monkey sex? I mean, with all the toys and harnesses needed to complete the task."

"That's why we chose your room…you already have the wires and hooks in place."

"Okay…stop." Her mom's hands waved between the girls. "I can only pretend for so long before I start seeing visuals and you both being virgins keeps me sane."

Becca eyed her black tipped French manicure and mumbled, "You'll never get quality anti-psychotics with that outlook."

Chapter Eight

"Falling in love and having relationships are two different things."
—*Keanu Reeves*

Tightening her cleats, Sarah scanned the parking lot at the edge of the baseball field. She knew Ashton would be there, but she wanted to see Karen, hopefully before her mother showed up. It's not that Sarah was trying to ambush Karen, but her mother's opinion always meant a lot to her.

"Hey Lesibatron," Becca said as she came from behind the bleachers. "So where's the woman of the year?"

"Not here yet," Sarah grumbled. "Why are you here?"

"Sisterly support and all."

Sarah arched her eyebrow at Becca.

"I'm here for you. The last thing you want is gushy mcgusherton saying the wrong thing in public. You think I should start dropping my birth control into her coffee? Would that stabilize her hormones?"

"What would I know about menopause?"

"Isn't that what you all talk about in your knitting circles or when you're rebuilding an engine?"

"I missed the last meeting."

"What meeting?" Sarah's mother asked as she approached while fumbling with her keys.

Maybe she was going through menopause. She looked frazzled, hot, and irritated. Then again, she'd just spent ten minutes in the car with Becca.

"Holy shit," Becca exclaimed.

"Becca, language," their mother chided only to have the same reaction. "Holy shit."

Sarah turned to see what had gotten both of the women's attention. Ashton. He really did have that effect on the breeders. At least it confirmed with Sarah that Karen had to be gay as the day is long to not be drooling if her own mother was about to drop her panties.

"That's my girl...who he has his arm around, since I'm assuming you haven't made it past his biceps."

"There's a woman by him?" Becca asked, not taking her eyes off of Ashton, who was wearing a white, sleeveless, form fitting workout top that made his tan pop even more. Loose shorts hung from his hips and fell to his knees.

But all Sarah could see was Karen with her auburn hair pulled into a smooth ponytail and her arm also around Ash's waist. Although her blue shirt was short sleeved, it was still a starched button-up, and perfect khaki shorts finished her outfit.

"Sarah, right?" Ashton asked as they approached. "I was going to help out your team today. My name is Ashton."

He extended his hand and Sarah clenched her teeth.

"Yes, I believe we met briefly at the county fair."

"You're right. I met so many people that weekend."

Karen hadn't released her hand from Ash's hip and she was still practically glued to his side.

"Karen, right?" Sarah said as she extended her hand, forcing Karen to release Ash and shake.

"Yes, Karen Schroeder."

"Well, this is my mother Patty, Patty Lindstrom, and my sister Becca."

Karen was cordial and shook hands. Gabbie showed up with a uniform for Ash and Case growling behind her.

"The doctor said it was okay. He said it would be fine."

"Until someone tries to slide into home."

Mary Beth joined Sarah and gave her the dirty eyeball.

"You didn't play when you were pregnant," Sarah said to Mary Beth, trying to stay out of Case's earshot.

85

"I was showing."

"Good point."

"No, it's not," Case snapped at the two of them.

"What's the problem?" Patty asked.

Gabbie looked panic stricken as she gazed at her mother.

"Oh, just tell her," Sarah said, then turned to her mom. "It's early…but Gabbie's…"

A squeal of delight pierced the eardrums of most in the metro area as the overly emotional Patty bear hugged Gabbie.

"You think she figured it out?" Becca teased with her arms crossed. "Where'd your girlfriend go?"

Karen was standing by the porta-pottys holding Ashton's bag. What the hell?

"Could she be less into you?"

"She's into me. Trust me. I'm sure she's just nervous."

"I'd hold on to that piece of ass if I was scared, too. Damn, I'm not into older guys, but he's—"

"Yeah, I got it," Sarah snapped as she stormed to the dugout.

"What's going on?" Mary Beth asked as she tucked her hair into her cap.

"Nothing."

The best thing about a best friend is they're always there for you, the worst thing… they expect you to always need them. Right now Mary Beth wasn't going to let Sarah get away with her comment.

"Karen won't take her hands off Ashton."

Mary Beth scanned the field and settled in on the sight Sarah couldn't stand.

"She doesn't feel him up that much when they're on the campaign trail. Why is she acting like a weak little woman?"

"I don't think that's what she's going for."

"Then what?"

"Ash is hot, like mega hot. I'd be glued to him to keep the skanks off him, too."

"She doesn't care if he sleeps with other women."

"And he doesn't care if she does, but this is her game. She's played it for a decade now. They know what they're doing."

"Who's here to out them? Seriously? There aren't any reporters."

"But there are probably thirty cell phones with access to every social media source out there."

"I just wanted her to meet my mom."

Mary Beth rocked back on her heels, then fell forward against the gate, blocking the dugout. Her fingers curled around the steel diamonds as she looked out across the field.

"What did you really think would happen? She'd meet Patty and suddenly realize the world is fair? She'd rush to embrace you because now she gets that a closet isn't a place to live."

"When she's with me I feel like I'm in a relationship, now I feel like a fool."

"Look, she's sitting by your mom and Gabbie now." Mary Beth snapped to attention. "Oh hell no."

"What?"

"Case looks like he thinks he's playing."

"No." Sarah turned and saw Case adjusting Gabbie's catcher's mask and protective chest padding. There was no way he'd be able to wear that, let alone catch one of Mary Beth's pitches. "We're so dead."

It was then Ashton walked up to Case, pulled gear out of his bag and Case was smiling. They shook hands and Case walked to the dugout.

"Thank God for that new guy. I'll be playing second," he said.

"Our season is over," Sarah sighed.

"Now don't say that, he might be good." Mary Beth tilted her head to the side. "At least he has gear that fits."

"If you bean him in the head a few times I won't be mad," Mandy said as she plopped her bag down. "It wouldn't hurt him. He's already got permanent brain damage."

"Not wanting to watch the latest episode of Wives of Rockers kinda makes me think he doesn't have brain damage," Sarah retorted.

As the rest of the team showed up, Sarah kept looking at Karen who didn't even glance her way. This was embarrassing. Sarah's confessed her love for Karen only to have her act as if they'd never met.

* * * *

Patty eyed Karen, who had a pit in her stomach from the moment

Ashton pulled up in the parking lot. What was she thinking? Suddenly she realized she couldn't give Sarah a hug. They didn't even have a story about how Ashton ended up playing with this random team. Karen kept her phone at the ready knowing she'd be fielding calls from the office through the whole game. She wanted to support Sarah, but wasn't sure how she could do that.

"Do you usually come to the games?" Karen asked, thinking it wasn't school ball. Why would a mother come to an adult game?

"No, I was invited. My daughter wanted me to meet someone."

"Oh…" Karen's face flushed with heat and she closed her eyes. If she looked around she might see someone or something that would make her run. Her stomach churned and she reached for the bottle of water in her purse.

"Although I don't know how I can find out about a person who's limited on what she can talk about." Patty extended her legs and crossed them at the ankle. "I love my daughter, and I wish her the utmost happiness. No matter what her path is in life, I'll support it. Sadly, I know some parents aren't like that. It must be hard."

"It is."

"Sarah doesn't understand that. Right now I can see she's upset. Hurt even."

Karen looked to third base and Sarah, who was warming up by tossing the ball between Mandy and Case.

"Daddy keeps dropping Mama," a little girl who'd been introduced as Claire said to Gabbie.

"I know," Gabbie said as she covered her eyes. "He's trying, so we need to cheer him on anyway."

"Maybe the ball's too small. You thinks they'd let him use his basketball?"

"No honey, hopefully Daddy will figure it out before your Aunties have to beat him up."

"They should," Claire said as she crossed her arms. "Why he stoppin' you from playin'?"

"Mama's not feeling too good right now. He's just trying to help out."

"You gots a belly ache?" Claire asked her mother.

"Something like that." Gabbie rubbed her belly protectively with a sly smile.

Three innings into the game Karen felt something she'd not felt in years. Relaxed. Sure, she'd taken a half dozen phone calls about a stance on this or schmoozing with a potential donor, but after she hung up, there was always a place for her to sit without fifty questions.

"It must be hard," a man's voice came from behind her as she stood behind the bleachers. She'd just fielded a phone call from Howard and hadn't noticed the man approach. He wore jeans and a polo, but one that had seen it's time in the wash cycle enough that he didn't stand out as over dressed.

"Excuse me?"

"Balancing work and a love life."

"It can be, but when the person you're with is worth it you don't notice as much."

"You know what I found strange?"

"What's that?"

"You cheer louder for the third baseman than your fiancé."

Karen caught a chill as she looked along the third base line where Sarah had her legs spread and slightly bent. She punched her glove a few times as she eyed the person up to bat.

"She's having an impressive game," Karen said, although she was having problems with a suddenly desert-like mouth.

"Not really."

"Can I help you with something?" She asked as she stiffened. "If not I really need to go back."

"Yes Representative, you can," the man said as he fished a notepad out of his back pocket. "How did your fiancé get on this team?"

"I'm not really sure, he's the one with the free time, not me. If that's all…" Karen started to walk away.

"Which one of you is sleeping with her?"

"Who?"

"The third basemen."

"How dare you suggest—"

"I did my research, Representative. You go to her apartment at least three times a week with Ashton. Now, she has a roommate, one who's a

89

pretty big slut from all I've heard, but something tells me you're the one who's with the blonde."

"I have no idea what you're talking about."

"Why do you go there?"

"You need to direct all your questions to my campaign manager. I will not be insulted like this."

"What's insulting?" he called as she turned. "That I'd suggest you were a lesbian, or that you just like to hang out with them?"

"I have no idea what her sexual orientation is," Karen spat as she came at the reporter, who back-peddled in fear. "Nor is it my place to ask. Even worse, it is not yours and I'd thank you to leave."

"It's a public park."

"Yes," a voice came from behind Karen. "It is, but it does need to be cleaned up a bit."

Karen looked over her shoulder to see Gabbie with a softball bat in her hands. She let the end of it bounce in the palm of her hand. Behind her Karen saw Gabbie's father holding Claire who was very interested in her mother's actions.

"Have you met Representative Schroeder's security detail?" Gabbie asked as she flipped the bat down and used it as a cane to lean on. "Representative, Patty wanted that recipe you were talking about."

"Well, Mister...I'm sorry you never introduced yourself before berating me." Karen crossed her arms and the reporter scowled.

"Porter. Roger Porter."

"Well, Mr. Porter, I'm sorry, but one of my constituents needs me."

Karen walked back to the front of the bleachers and sat. Her hands trembled as she tried to hold her phone steady.

"I've got that," Gabbie said as she took the phone and swiped the screen to unlock it. "You know, being a politician, you should probably have a lock code on this."

"I know," Karen replied. "Thank you for that."

"We're a tight group. Family. We'll fight with each other, but no one messes with one of us. What did he want anyway?"

"He wanted to know if Ash or I were sleeping with Sarah."

"Oh." Gabbie sat back and pulled her son Charlie on her lap. "He didn't ask about Mandy?"

"She was brought up, but why would I bring my fiancé to his girlfriend's home?"

"Right. So what are you going to do?"

"We weren't sure if we were being followed. I've been taking too many chances."

"There must be a reason for that."

Sarah scooped up a grounder and whipped it to Mandy who tagged the runner with ease. They headed back to the dugout and Sarah's face had a worried furrow to it when she looked at Karen. Gabbie gave a small wave, but Sarah still seemed concerned.

"I chose this life," Karen confessed. "Have you ever made the wrong choice?"

"I'm human," Gabbie replied. "But very few choices are permanent."

Karen flashed to her family and what would happen if they found out. Could they accept her? Could she live without their acceptance? More importantly, could she live with herself if she stayed untrue to herself and the woman she loved? Every inch of Sarah had become important to her. The sound of her voice, the smell of her hair, and the feel of her hand on Karen's body.

"I'm not sure how to get out of where I am." Karen's eyes stayed locked on the field. "I've promised Sarah November, after the election, but that reporter..." Karen bristled in fear. "God, this game is going to take forever."

Karen buried her face in her hands until she felt someone gently rubbing circles in between her shoulder blades.

"Sarah just remembers me accepting her choice, she never remembers the stress before," Patty said. "My child was in pain and I couldn't figure out why. There were times when I swore she held her breath for hours."

Karen held in the tears that came to the surface as her throat burned in pain.

"When I realized why she felt different, I couldn't understand her fear, but it was real to her, so I helped her verbalize her feelings and it was like a stone had been lifted from her back. She became confident and the light returned to her eyes."

"I envy that light. I'm drawn to it like a ship lost at sea."

"The choice has to be yours and yours alone, but the sooner you steer to the lighthouse, the better you'll feel."

"But—"

Patty stopped rubbing her back and placed her hands on her lap.

"In mining communities they know going into the mine will eventually kill them. Black lung, cave in…it could be anything, but they do it because they can't see another way. They don't believe they have any option." She sighed and looked over at Sarah in the dugout. "When Sarah told me she was giving up her scholarship to open a daycare center I wanted to kill her. She'd be trapped all because her best friend got pregnant. It didn't make sense to me."

Gabbie bowed her head and sucked in her lips.

"I was scared she was throwing away her life. Maybe at first the girls didn't have a clear path."

"Well… yeah," Gabbie conceded, then got a few kisses as Claire ran by before lapping the bleacher again.

"They found one, one that makes me so proud of each of them. They are successful and happy." Just then Mandy slammed her bat against the gate and used it to threaten Ashton. "Well…most of them are happy."

"Did he try to take her batting position?" Gabbie asked. "That man has a death wish."

"Yes he does," Karen said as she looked over at the reporter standing by a tree watching the whole interaction.

"There is one thing I'm going to say," Patty became serious. "If you want to stay hidden, don't pull my daughter back in the shadows with you. She's found land and is better for it."

* * * *

Karen grabbed Ashton before Sarah even got out of the dugout. They practically ran to his car. What the hell happened?

"Ash probably can't play with us again," Gabbie sighed as she eyed Case who was pulling off the cleats he'd wasted money on. Sadly, aptitude in one sport doesn't mean you're an athlete. Now they'd need two new players if he kept insisting Gabbie can't play.

"Good," Mandy grumbled as she tossed her bats into her bag. "He was…well, sure he had…I don't like him."

"At least you didn't try to say he sucked, because if it wasn't for him covering home we'd have been creamed," Mary Beth joined the conversation. "He's an okay catcher, but I could tell he hated slow pitch."

"What happened?" Sarah finally asked. "Why did they sprint out of here?"

"Oh," Gabbie said. "That, well—"

"Excuse me, Ms. Lindstrom," a strange man in jeans and a polo approached, and Gabbie snatched a bat out of Mandy's open bag.

"Did you not get the hint earlier?"

"Gabbie, honey," Case sighed as he approached and took the bat from her. "Giving birth in shackles can't be comfortable. Let me kill him…but tell me why first."

"Fine," the man put his hands up in surrender. "I'll leave, but you can't hide forever."

He walked to the parking lot and no one spoke until he drove off.

"Why am I hiding?" Sarah asked.

"He's why Karen left. He's a reporter."

"Oh."

"I think she would have left in the third inning if Ashton hadn't been playing."

"I should call her."

"No," Patty said as she brushed some dirt off Sarah's face like she was a child. "Give her time. There are things she needs to sort out. You'll be a distraction. Let this be her choice, not her guilt."

"Mom, you don't understand."

"I know she has a primary in less than three weeks. Between now and then she has rallies, the state fair, and a big debate. All of which she needs to focus on if she's to win. Give her space right now."

"I'm not crowding her. I haven't been complaining that I never get to see her. I understand her job is time consuming."

"Then also understand you can't help her with her job. Not right now. Maybe in the future, but right now you'll bring her down."

"Down. Right. I'm the destroyer of all." Sarah trembled as she tried to cork her rage.

"And the PMS train has pulled into the station," Becca said as she pulled an imaginary whistle. "Toot, toot."

"I hope it doesn't jump track and run you over," Patty teased.

"It's not PMS," Sarah growled. It was humiliation. The anger that instead of Karen's arm around her waist she had her mother's patronizing glare…no, she didn't. Her mother's eyes were consoling.

"Is it too late for ice cream?" Patty asked when she looked at the yawning Charlie who stopped mid yawn at the offer.

"Mama?" he asked with droopy eyes. "Can we gets some ice scream?"

"Some ice scream? Is that when I drop it?" Gabbie asked.

"Cr…cre…cream. Ice cream," Charlie asked again.

"Sure, a cone wouldn't hurt," Case offered and Gabbie complied.

"Is the beast gone?" Mandy asked as she dropped her bag by the group.

"Yes, Ashton took off with Karen in a mad dash to avoid the lesbian," Sarah grumbled and received a dirty look from her mother.

"That makes sense." Mandy picked her bag back up and hefted it over her shoulder. "Did I hear someone say ice cream?"

"Dat was me, Auntie Mand," Charlie chimed in without the hint of exhaustion he'd had before the discussion had come up.

Sarah stewed in her own anger as she threw on a happy face for her friends while they laughed and ate ice cream. Luckily a new place had opened up with homemade ice cream and they had pistachio, which now Case and Eli had both acquired a taste for.

"When did this start?" she asked, holding up a spoonful of hard packed ice cream.

"When did what start?" Mary Beth asked as she passed her son Luke a wet wipe.

"Pistachio ice cream? It's not like it's a normal flavor."

"My…our brother Will," Mary Beth quickly corrected as she looked at Mandy who gave her a shrug telling her I-don't-give-a-fuck. "Mom had bought one of those Neapolitan packs with pistachio instead of strawberry because he was allergic to strawberries."

"That's right," Gabbie chimed in. "And Mandy loved mint chocolate chip so she scooped a huge chunk of it."

Sarah burst out in laughter when she remembered Mandy's initial face when she took a bite.

"I thought Mandy was going to throw up everywhere."

"Hey, when you expect mint and get nut flavored, it throws you off."

"But how could you spit out the most wonderful concoction known to man?" Gabbie sighed and placed a spoonful in her mouth.

"Well, I don't spit it out now."

"Personal life aside," Becca teased, Sarah's mom blushed, and the rest of the girls fell into a fit of laughter.

You were amazing tonight. Sorry I couldn't stay. Emergency at the office. Love you.

The text didn't come until later, after Sarah had already gotten into her car. She tried to console herself that it was enough.

Chapter Nine

"Control your own destiny or someone else will."
—*Jack Welch*

"I want him banned from all my public appearances." Karen stormed at Howard who had come over on Karen's command.

He was sitting next to Ashton watching Karen's arms flail as she paced back and forth in her living room. She'd barely been home in the last month due to having meetings in Sarah's bedroom via phone at night. Dust had started to settle on her book shelves and coffee table where a decorative set of glass balls sat in the middle of a hand woven basket. Did that even go together? It must, Howard wasn't complaining about her style choices this week.

"You do understand the word public, correct?" Howard patronized.

"What did you find out about Roger Porter?" She growled. "It's been at least two hours since I sent you his name."

"Freelancer, has been published in everything from blogs and local papers to *The New York Times*. I'm not sure if he was sent to cover you or he smelled blood in the water."

"What does he usually write about?"

"He's a gossip guy," Howard replied. "He's credited with a few dozen sex scandals."

"I'm not a sex scandal."

"You are cheating on me with a woman," Ashton added as he leaned back and stretched. "After all I've done for you."

"Well, maybe if your dick was good enough, I wouldn't have to

96

wander," Karen snapped.

"Ouch." Ashton crinkled his nose. "Don't insult the equipment because you like latex and manmade better. For all you know, your favorite toy might be made from a mold of mine."

"That's more horrific than the thought of sleeping with you." Karen placed her right hand over her eyes and wrapped her left arm around her stomach. "Can you shower? Seriously how could you work up an odor that bad in a few hours of slow pitch softball?"

"My manly musk brings all the girls to the yard." Ashton pushed up and raised his armpit by Karen's nose. "I'm only going to shower because I know how bitchy you get when deprived of your nightly orgasm when campaigning."

"What's that supposed to mean?"

"It means your new girlfriends only seem to pop up around campaign season, or haven't you noticed?"

"No they don't."

"Yes, they do," Howard added. "Which means either you're trying to sabotage yourself, or you need a partner to get you through the tough times. Maybe you should just get a good assistant."

"I want women other times of the year." Karen looked back and forth between Howard and Ashton. "Don't I?"

"I'm not in your wet dreams." Ashton sighed and gave her a kiss on her cheek. "You want me to spend the night just in case Porter's watching?"

"Yes," Karen responded, still stunned at the idea she only wanted women during campaign season. She tried to catalog her relationships. It was true. She was a campaign slut.

Now that Ashton was out of the room, Karen suddenly felt exposed with Howard sitting on her couch like her father.

"Sarah loves me."

"That sucks. Especially when you break her heart."

"I don't want to break her heart. I want her past the campaign."

"How would you know?"

"Because she's…it's different this time."

"You sure?" Howard asked. "Because every campaign you talk about outing yourself at one point or another."

"But I never gave the girl a date. Maybe this is my M.O., but Sarah's different."

"Are you?" Howard pushed up off the couch. "I'll try my hardest to deal with Roger Porter, but there's little I can do. Avoid her. Kiss Ashton on the way to the office. Hold his hand."

"I mean it," Karen said when Howard put his hand on her doorknob. "This is the last campaign I stay hidden."

"Sure it is."

Howard's glare and words dug in Karen's psyche. It invaded her dreams, causing her to thrash and reach for anything to quiet her mind. Sleep was like a hat blown off by the wind, always at the tip of her fingers, but another gust comes by and trips and bounces it further away.

Karen woke curled in Ashton's arm and snuggled against his chest. He was warm and she felt safe, but he was hard. Firm muscles and hair on his belly from his bellybutton to the top of his waistband. Worse yet, he was erect.

When she woke enough to be disgusted she rolled over and groaned. "Must you?"

"Huh," he groggily responded as he hit the alarm clock.

"Can't you control that thing?"

He looked down at the raised sheet and smiled.

"Take it as a compliment." His hand lazily went down his stomach and began to lift the sheet when Karen freaked.

"In the shower or your own home. You're not soiling my sheets with your DNA."

"I was just scratching. Trust me, you're not as hot as the woman I was dreaming about. I'm already at half-mast seeing your bed-head."

Karen immediately used her fingers to comb out her hair, and then flopped back on the bed in defeat.

"I was up half the night thanks to you."

"I crashed like a newborn and now I'm stiff as hell thanks to your girlfriend. Man, I'm old." Ash sat on the side of the bed and cracked his back as he stretched from side to side. "I shouldn't have said what I did. I didn't mean you weren't into girls."

"I'm a campaign whore. I need sex to release the stress. Otherwise I might as well be celibate."

"I beg to differ."

"Where were you at two-thirty this morning?"

"You need to relieve stress all year long." He turned and looked at her over his shoulder. "You're putting yourself in an early grave. Denying who you are is a major part of it, but you take on every bill like it's a personal cause. You devour every part of it and weigh the pros and cons. Sweetie, you're just one vote. An important one, but just one. Some of the legislation isn't worth your health."

"You think Porter started investigating when I voted for the same sex amendment."

"And you're ignoring me again."

"No...I'm just...I can't focus and I need to. This has me all discombobulated." Karen gathered herself and got back on track. "What crap do I have to do today?"

"You're single. Engaged to one of the hottest men in politics—"

"What do you do that's in politics?"

"I have a job in your office." He stood and moved the curtain in her window to peek outside.

"Is he out there?" Karen asked in fear.

"No, but your neighbor is," he purred.

"You mean my neighbor's daughter is outside."

"She's eighteen."

"And in her Catholic school uniform. You know for a religion that pushes chastity, they should know better than to put a woman in a short skirt and knee highs."

"You're an animal."

"What if it were Sarah in the same outfit?" He asked as his fingers released the soft, satin fabric of her curtain. "Is that a blush? Why Representative, maybe you are in love."

"Uh huh?"

"Say what you want, you never missed Astrid when she wasn't in the room."

"I...see I was...I didn't, did I?"

Ashton shrugged and returned to leering at the neighbor girl until Karen heard a bus show up a minute later.

"As far as your schedule, with only six days until the primary it's not going to be ugly." He reached for his t-shirt and yawned. "Last I checked we have five campaign stops starting with a brunch at a women's club."

"Five? Why do I want to do this again?"

"You're power hungry. Insatiable really."

"I am not."

"Then again, back to your health."

"Why are you so focused on my health?"

"I worry. You're looking exhausted and not eating right."

"It's hard to eat right when every other meal is fried."

"How about a run before we hit the trail? Exercise is a great way to break the monotony and release the stress of not having sex."

"It's been less than a day."

"For you maybe," Ashton grumbled.

"Aww, Ash, is someone having a dry spell?"

"While you're getting some I'm stuck with the psycho man hater."

"Mandy?" Karen let out a small laugh. "From what Sarah says, the last thing Mandy hates is men."

"At least you found another woman who can resist my charms."

"Have you been trying to charm her?" Karen teased.

"No, I know better than to arm wrestle with a grizzly bear."

Karen walked to her closet and with a swish she began moving the starched stiff business suits that seemed to define her life. All slightly varied, but in the same dull pallet.

"What events?" She asked again, hoping she could get away with a linen pantsuit.

"A variety of women's groups, educators, and public service professionals." Ashton went to his closet in her room and pulled out a pair of black pants and a button-up light blue shirt. His only choice was the color of his shirt. Karen envied the simplicity of his life. "Don't forget we're doing debate prep all week starting tonight."

"No one watches the local debates. Why does Howard harp on this so much?"

"It's good practice for later, when you're up against the Dem later in the season."

He poked his head out of his closet and tossed a pillow at her head so she turned.

"Don't forget...eventually it'll be for the presidency."

* * * *

Sarah flipped her phone between her fingers as if that would make it ding with a voicemail or text message. Stalking wasn't her favorite past time, and Karen had warned her this week she'd be a bit out of touch, but it had been two days since the softball game. With a loud sigh, she let the phone drop to the table and began spinning it like a top.

"You ready to go?" Mandy asked as she pulled her long, dark hair into a misshapen bun that still had hair unclaimed in the binder.

"Huh?" Sarah replied, knocked from her deep thoughts.

"Our supplies are all in. You know we're supposed to spend our days off and the weekends to set up our classrooms."

"Yeah, I know."

Mandy took the seat across from Sarah at the table.

"No word?"

"Not even a 'K' to my last text."

"That reporter must have really spooked her."

"I guess." Sarah rested her head on her hand with her elbow bent on the table. "It's just...I don't get it."

"What was that?" Mandy asked as she looked around the room and behind her back. "Can you hear it?"

"Hear what?" Sarah strained as she attempted to hear the strange sound.

"The 'told ya so' fairy. She's sprinkling told ya so dust everywhere."

"I hate you...I really, really hate you."

"I know, but um...told ya so." She then reached across the table and brushed her finger on Sarah's nose and Sarah slapped her away. "You had a little on your nose."

"I am dating a Republican, which means I now have my permit to carry," Sarah growled in warning.

"I call bullshit, but that was a good one." Mandy got up and poured the last of the coffee into a travel mug, then turned and leaned against the counter. "So, I assume a shower is out, but could you get out of your jammies?"

A half hour later, Sarah was unpacking polynomial squares and bead chains. Arranging each item in its place, she tried to let the day's work distract her. It's not like she didn't have tons to do also. She was busy and it was good that Karen wasn't clingy and in need of her constant attention and approval. Steeling her emotions away, Sarah tried to come to grips with the first major hiccup in the relationship. Not the first. Signs had been there all along, but she'd been blind to them. Just like always.

Even now, she craved Karen. She needed her arms to keep her warm. It was as bad as Lisa leaving. The person she wanted to hold her was the one who broke her heart. What was wrong with her?

Luke rushed into the room and jumped on her back.

"Hey Auntie Sarah," he cooed. "I can call you that when there isn't school right?"

"Yes sweetie." She patted his little arms around her neck.

Behind him, Mary Beth carried a fruit tray from a local supermarket and a pint of pistachio ice cream.

"I'm not that bad off." Sarah passed Luke a thousand and hundred cube so he could place them on their shelf.

"Not what I've heard." Mary Beth passed the ice cream and spoon to her. "I heard you've been unpacking the same box for the past hour."

"Have you ever put together the bead case?"

"No, but honey you're dating a very busy person. There will be times when you can't see her for weeks at a time."

"That doesn't make me feel better." Sarah lay back on the floor and stared at the ceiling. "Weeks?"

"You met her in the calm before the storm."

"If that was the calm I'm not going to handle the storm." Sarah looked at her friend right as her head got pulled into Mary Beth's lap. "A few times a week, and half the time she was on the phone or computer."

Mary Beth ran her fingers through Sarah's hair to soothe her. When Sarah closed her eyes she felt a tear escape. A hard lump formed in her throat as she turned and curled against Mary Beth's leg. She never cried for Lisa. She'd been shocked, but a part of her was relieved. Their relationship had come to a point where they needed to move it forward or end it. She chose the path she'd been raised to take. Her parents had had struggles, but always came through stronger than before. She had been raised to not give up on someone, but maybe this time she'd need to let go.

* * * *

"Representative, how do you plan to reform the current health care system?" Helen Miller asked her older sister.

Karen stood at the music stand they had used as a podium since Karen first ran for office in the eighth grade. She'd answered questions from cafeteria food to the global debt crisis. How more seasoned did she have to be? Between debate club and over twenty elections, she had stock answers for every conceivable question.

"Did you forget?" Helen groaned. "Oversight on spending costs with the facilities as well as insurance companies. Blah, blah, bullshit, bullshit political jargon. Then pull out the history on Walter and how he wants to punish poor people and let them all die on the steps of the ER."

"It really is so predictable."

"From what I've had to endure." Helen sighed and leaned back in their father's recliner.

Helen was the middle sister of the Schroeder brood and the only one who'd help with debate prep anymore. Howard and Ashton eyed her as she began to pout. They were in their third hour for the fourth day in a row. She'd answered the question probably fifteen times.

"All right," Howard said. "I'm calling it."

"Thank God," Ashton groaned as he got up and stretched. "I was going to gnaw my arm off if I didn't get some of your mom's stroganoff."

"You only stay with me for my mother's food."

"What else do you have that would have me coming back for more?" Ash asked as he pulled Karen into his arms and rubbed her stiff lower back.

"Please," her sister grumbled. "You two can barely keep your hands off each other. I'd be surprised if you haven't worn out a half dozen beds since high school."

Helen left the room and Howard scowled at the two of them.

"What did we do now?" Karen asked, straining the word now because Ash had dug into a huge knot and the sensation from pain turned into a sweet release of pressure.

"If he gets you off that much why can't that be enough?" Howard asked.

Ash immediately stopped massaging, and Karen's eyes snapped open.

"Howard, I'm going to say this as nicely as I can," Ash began, and Karen could feel the tears in the corner of her eyes. "She loves Sarah. God willing, she'll be able to stay with her. Stop trying to fit a triangle into a square hole. It doesn't work."

"Maybe if your dick wasn't oblong it could do the job."

"If my dick was a pussy it might do the job."

"Stop," Karen yelled. "I'm tired. I'm sorry I'm not the candidate you want. I'm just the candidate you have."

"Oh Karen, quit being so dramatic," her mother said as she entered the room with two plates of stroganoff. "It was one question, and you'll remember it when it's important. Howard has loved and supported you from the day you were born." She ran her hand along the edge of Karen's face and cradled it as if she were still a little girl. "You're just hungry, get a little food in your belly and you'll be on point again."

"Your mom's cooking could turn anyone into the next President of the United States," Ashton teased as he dug into his food.

"Oh Ash, you're going to be a wonderful First Husband." All but Karen laughed at the joke. "That is if you ever get up the nerve to actually ask her officially to marry you."

"Yeah Ash," Howard goaded. "Why haven't you dropped to one knee for Karen? It could be a great way to end her debate."

"Now you ruined any surprise," her mother chided. "Howard, you have all the romance of a national convention."

Karen pushed some food around on her plate. "That's because Howard only cares about the public image and not what I want."

"You need to go back stage next time at the national, it's more romantic than you think," Howard grumbled.

"Don't you want to marry Ash?" her mother asked, and Karen caught a chill.

When she looked into her mother's caramel eyes Karen felt the full weight of her lies. She could see the hope in her mother's eyes and even though acid burned up and scratched at her throat, she gave the stock answer she'd had memorized since she was a child.

"Of course I do."

Chapter Ten

"There is nothing like returning to a place that remains unchanged to find the ways in which you yourself have altered."
—*Nelson Mandela*

The night before the debate Karen lay in her childhood bed and stared at the ceiling. Her phone buzzed and she reached for it hoping for Sarah, but it wasn't her throw away phone—that had mysteriously gone missing—it was her regular one.

"Yes," she groaned as she rolled out of bed and put on her slippers.

"I knew you wouldn't be asleep," Ash knowingly said.

"It's a stock response, to a stock phone call."

"Hey, it's not a stock phone call."

"Okay, you didn't call before the student council elections senior year."

"There was a reason for that...I believe her name was Carmen."

"Carmen Donnelly. You're such a slut." Karen pulled on her robe and tied the sash.

"You're jealous."

"Not really, just once I wish..."

"That a girl knew you're always up at three thirty the night before a debate. Worse yet, you run home to sleep."

Karen sighed and headed out the French doors to the deck.

"I miss her." She padded down the stone path to the dock and took off her slippers.

"That's not stock," Ash replied.

"I know, I've made a decision." Karen dipped her toes into the cool

106

lake.

"You know Howard hates when you do that on your own."

"Only in election years. The rest of the time I'm actually allowed to govern."

"What's your decision, oh leader of the free world?"

"After the debate, I'm coming out to my family."

"The Schroeders? You have met your family, right? Their undying devotion to you might just waver."

"I'm an adult. I can survive on my own."

"Says the woman who runs to mommy and daddy's when she needs to get balanced."

"But I'm not...even here I'm not balanced. Worse yet, I feel like an outsider. Like I don't belong anymore."

"When did that start?"

"The first time I came by after I met Sarah." Karen kicked at the water. "Everyone was here with their husbands and I wasn't."

"I was there."

"But *she* wasn't."

"When was the last time you spoke to her?"

"The softball game." A pit formed in the center of her chest. Pressure burned against her sternum and she pressed hard with the heel of her hand to dull the pain. "I may be having a heart attack. I'm not too young you know."

"Lesbians don't have heart attacks, something about all the pussy in their diet. That's why I try my best to get a serving a day."

"You're not funny."

"But I am adorable," Ashton sighed. "Back to you, my love...the softball game. You didn't really speak to her there."

"I know." Soreness ate its way up her throat and she clawed at her knee. "Would you please check on her? Make sure I'm still good with her."

"Why can't you?"

"I think Howard stole my throw away and he thinks Porter's tapping everything. I probably shouldn't be talking to you right now."

"I'll see what I can find out before the debate."

"Thank you. Um, Ash..." Karen nibbled on her bottom lip. "I love her. I don't want to give her up. It's different this time. I'd give up everything if I knew I could wake up in bed next to her every morning."

"Her?" Karen jumped at the sound of her sister Darlene's voice.

"I gotta go, Ash."

"Karen, Karen what happened?" Ashton's voice had changed from his normal calm demeanor.

"Darlene's here."

"Oh shit, what did she hear?"

"I'll talk to you later, love you, Ash." Karen hit end and placed the phone in her robe pocket. "Hey Dar, couldn't you sleep?"

Darlene flopped on the bench they had on the side of the dock and rested her elbows on her knees. She was wearing a pair of pink flannel pajama bottoms and white camisole. Her hair was a shade darker than Karen's. It was best described as chestnut, and fashioned into a short bob. Karen was glad in the dark she couldn't see her youngest sister's eyes.

"I left my new husband to come and help with your debate prep."

"Thank you for that," Karen replied, not really sure what Darlene did outside of whining about doing dishes.

"I wasn't done."

"Okay."

"Now you were pretending to talk to Ashton—"

"I was talking to Ash." Karen held up her phone, but Darlene shook it off.

"Who is she?"

"She?" Karen replied innocently.

"The woman you'd give up everything to sleep next to."

"I don't understand the question."

"Why haven't you married Ash? You've been together for over a decade."

"You never cared before."

"I never heard my sister say she would give up everything. You've devoted yourself to public service. I've been in more parades than a convertible. Tell me the truth," Darlene steeled herself and swallowed hard. "Are you not marrying Ash because you're a lesbian?"

For years Karen could have answered without a second thought.

Scoffing at such an inconceivable notion. Then she realized she'd never been asked about her sexual preference. Nasty comments and sneers following her vote last year, but never had she been asked straight out.

Karen opened her mouth to answer, but nothing came out. She couldn't lie to her sister...actually any of her family members. Of course, they wouldn't ask if she was gay. Her sexuality, like her party affiliation, was assumed. The opposite wouldn't even enter their mind. Unlike Sarah's mom, Karen's couldn't see the pain her daughter was in as she struggled with her urges.

"Wow," Darlene let out a gust of air, and Karen swore she was having a heart attack from the pressure. "You finally make sense to me."

"What?" scratched out of Karen's throat.

"I knew you couldn't be that much of a power hungry bitch."

"Um...thank you." Maybe Karen was imagining her sister's reaction? That explained her lightheaded feeling and the fact she hadn't been doused in gasoline to be burned at the stake. "You're not mad?"

"Mad...no, but I am disappointed. I know I'm the baby, but we've always been close."

"Because I changed your diapers?"

"No, just because you helped me with a lot of firsts. We've talked about everything. You're the only one who I told about trying to get pregnant. Why couldn't you tell me you were questioning your sexuality?"

"It was never a question," Karen admitted. "I tried to deny my feelings and until...until Sarah I didn't care about it."

"Sarah? That's your first girlfriend? Are you sure—"

"She's not my first."

Darlene inhaled sharply and sat back as if Karen had slapped her.

"I could compartmentalize my life and act like someone holding me didn't matter."

"How many women have you been with?"

"How many guys have you slept with?"

"This isn't about me." Darlene became defensive. "Sex with guys isn't—"

"That many," Karen chided as she felt the pressure begin to release in her chest.

"Kare Bear, I'm being serious. How do you know you're gay?"

"Because even Ashton, who I love more than warm banana bread, can't get me wet."

"TMI." Darlene waved her hands and closed her eyes.

"When I'm with a woman I feel right. I feel…"

Karen looked at her sister and for the first time she could verbalize her feelings. Then again this was the first time she'd been asked outright.

"When Carter walks in the room can you feel it?"

"Feel what?"

"His presence. When you smell his cologne on his shirts, do you feel safe? When he places his hand on yours, do you warm?"

"He's one person. By your standards you're in love with a woman, not women."

"I'm not a slut, but fine. A hot guy takes off his shirt. Do you drool and think I wanna get me some of that?"

"I'm a married woman."

Karen crossed her arms and scowled at her sister.

"If you don't want to know, don't ask. Seriously. I'm gay. I know I am just like you know you're not. I'd marry Ash tomorrow if I could give myself to him, but I can't. Not really. He's my best friend, but there's no attraction."

"And this girl…she's…" Darlene struggled to find an explanation for her sister's strange behavior. "How long?"

"Sarah? Not long."

"How long have you known?"

"Junior high, high school, I don't know. I've never been interested in guys."

"Who knows?"

"A handful of people. Sarah has friends that seem to be in her business…" Darlene stared and Karen knew it didn't matter what she did, this was an unexplainable flaw. She might as well reveal she was defecting to Russia. Actually, turning Communist would probably make more sense to her family. "Dar, I…I'm having a hard time right now, please don't make it worse."

"When I lie it makes it hard to breathe, is that your problem?"

"Something like that."

"Then stop."

* * * *

A full week had passed. Sarah had no communication with Karen, and as much as she wanted to crawl into a hole and die, her friends did what they do when any of them were in pain. They rallied. Even if she wanted to be alone, she couldn't. It was like they scheduled shifts to be in her presence. Mandy even crawled in bed next to her at night. Besides being a cover hog and prone to kicking, Mandy had never been the person she wanted next to her in bed. But it was sweet and her horrible taste in reality TV shows did keep Sarah distracted.

"Ms. Sarah?" Theo approached her. "I finished my work. Can you check?"

"Yes, what were you working on today?"

"I did...um...I counted to a thousand."

"All by yourself?"

"No...um, Max worked with me, too."

"All right."

Sarah had her notebook and looked around the room. In the corner Jasmine was giving a lesson with the movable alphabet. The rest of the children were focusing on their task. Everything from cleaning small metal objects, to a world puzzle and reading books. In here she was exempt from her pain. The children kept her focused and her personal problems were taken completely off the stove.

In the hallway, a long, thin rug had been laid out. On it was the thousand chain with number markers all along the side. Max hopped up and clapped his little hands. The boys showed the big numbers they had counted to.

"How many days have you been working on this?" Sarah asked. "I've seen this in the hallway for a few days now."

"Um...since..." Max reached for the days of the week in his head. "What's the second day?"

"Tuesday. The second day you come here?"

"Yes, Tuesday."

"Two days of hard work, have you boys even had a break?"

"We had a snack," Theo said.

111

"This is impressive work, boys." Sarah smiled. "A thousand in two days. I know older children that can't work that fast."

She noted the achievement in her notebook and enjoyed a moment with the boys whose eyes beamed with pride.

"Now you guys have the really hard part, you have to put your work away."

"What about my mommy?" Max asked.

"Mommies don't clean up after big boys like you."

"I wanted her to see it."

"Hmm…maybe we should take a picture to send her. Do you think that would work?"

"Can my mommy get it, too?" Theo asked.

"Yes. Let me get my camera." Sarah turned toward her classroom and saw Ashton standing in the hallway. "You know what, boys? How about you get a snack so I can talk to our visitor, and then I'll take your picture after."

The boys were about to protest, but Sarah gave the teacher look and they returned to the classroom.

"Are you here to clean up?"

"You know my mommy cleans up my messes," Ashton teased and extended his hand toward a bench in the hallway.

Sitting down, Sarah tried to stamp down her anger that he was here. Growing Strong was her safe place. The exempt place where she didn't have to feel the hurt she did at home.

"How have you been?"

"I let my last girlfriend drag things out. I didn't face the truth. Ash, I hang on longer than I should."

"Is that what you think is happening here?"

"A week of silence." Sarah swallowed the lump that had reappeared. "I don't want to be clingy, but I need acknowledgement that I exist."

"I think that's why I'm here. Howard stole her phone with your number. Outside of public appearances, she's been in lockdown at her family's home."

A flutter of hope ran through her body, but there was something in Ashton's voice that was a warning.

"Sarah, right now she's so damn torn. What she says she'll be doing and what will really happen…I can't make any promises."

"What am I to her? In my mind, we were a couple. She was my girlfriend."

"Was?"

Wasn't that the question of the day? Sarah took in Ashton's perfectly formed jaw and body structure. She'd seen the press coverage of Karen this week. She'd been tucked in his strong arms. Karen's arm seemed to be glued to his hip. Every day she'd been "caught" smooching with Ash. Sure, he was her beard to hide who was in her heart, but Sarah understood now what Mandy had been saying. If Karen cannot love herself from the inside out, she was incapable of loving Sarah.

"Yes." Sarah turned to Ashton. "Was."

* * * *

The green room at the community center for the debate might as well be a cage at a zoo. All the classrooms in the center had glass walls and, even with moving two white boards by the one to the hallway, everyone could peer in. On the side Karen could see Walter.

He was older and had towed the company line for years. A veteran who'd actually been in a war, he had a sterner look to him. Rugged, tawny skin with bright blue eyes. Karen could tell that when he was younger he was handsome. He wore a navy blue suit with a bright red tie. Karen had the luxury of being able to wear the power color on her whole suit. With a high collar that she'd attempted to adjust for the thousandth time to get air, she smoothed out her skirt and prepared to slide on her comfortable, but classic black heels.

Ashton opened the door with a hermetically sealed sounding pop. Wringing her hands, she walked still barefoot toward him. The look on his face told her more than any words could. He smiled, but not in his eyes. It was his calm—the crazy politician look.

"You ready?" he asked as he kissed her forehead.

"What did she say?" Karen asked as she stared at the small red polka dots on his blue tie. She couldn't look him in the eye. Then he could lie and tell her it would all be fine. The fear she had was all for naught. "Lie to me if you have to."

The words fell from her lips like blood dripping from an open wound. Holding on until the liquid was too heavy to stay attached to the injury and had to break free and shatter on the ground. Karen needed the lies to keep her in the room. To keep her focused on the task at hand. She knew what she needed to keep going. No matter the cost, the lie could get her through the next hour. Then she could have the truth. When she had time to recover in private. Not here in the fishbowl with reporters circling as if they'd just chummed the waters.

"Everything is fine. I explained that Howard stole your phone and you've been on lockdown."

All good excuses, except she wouldn't accept them from a girlfriend, so how could she expect Sarah to? All her relationships had been one sided.

"Five minutes, Representative." A young man poked his head through the door wearing a headset.

"Thank you," she called back. "Guess it's time."

She reached for her heels, and then a bottle of water. At first she wasn't able to grip the top due to her trembling hands. Ashton reached for it and she swatted his hand away. With a deep breath, she closed her eyes, moved her head side to side, and twisted the top off. When she opened her eyes, she looked through those in front of her. Unfocused, she gazed into the other room, but even that didn't have her attention. She'd gone into the zone, the world she lived in alone. Always alone. Her family would sit dutifully in the front two rows. Her siblings, now married and having children, expanded her cheering section. Ashton would hold her hand and make sure she hit the mark set by Howard, but they weren't who she needed.

In Sarah's bedroom, Karen had found a connection strong enough to remove her from such a crazy world. That room was a sanctuary where she could melt into a person. Sex aside, the moments she treasured the most were their conversations. They connected on levels she'd heard were possible, but never understood. Years passed between true smiles brought on by joy, but crossing the threshold to Sarah's apartment stripped away the false world she was forced to inhabit.

Ashton placed his hand on her shoulder and her eyes calibrated to judge the room around her. More importantly, she saw Walter talking to Roger Porter. They both turned to look directly at her. He knew.

In that moment, she had a choice to make. Did she turn and practically rape Ashton right then and there to prove she wasn't in love with a beautiful, blonde teacher with breasts, curves, and lips that she couldn't get enough of? Or did she step on stage and change her life?

Chapter Eleven

"Anyone can hide. Facing up to things, working through them, that's what makes you strong."
—*Sarah Dessen*

"I heard Ash stopped by today," Mandy said as she sat next to Sarah, who thought she'd escaped her babysitters by sneaking to the park across from the school. "There was the smell of testosterone and too much male grunting to be Eli or Case."

"Yep," she sighed and watched the Canadian geese pecking at the ground by the lake. The sun was on its descent, but still over the trees. Reflecting off the placid lake, Sarah had been trying to silence her mind.

"It's over?"

"I guess," she shrugged. "I kind of ended it I suppose."

"You? You don't end things."

"She was just a booty call. You wanted me to have random orgasms."

"Oh Sarah," Mandy sighed and placed her arm around Sarah's shoulders and squeezed. "I love you girl, but we both know you can't do that. Plus, you don't have them come back day after day."

"It was my first time. Don't worry, the next girl I'll kick out without cuddling."

"I dare to dream." Mandy rested her head on Sarah's shoulder and Sarah wrapped her arm around Mandy's waist.

She loved that her friends would always be there to keep her going. Who did Karen have? Ash? He helped her, but it helped him, too. Karen had told her more women came on her campaign to sleep with Ash than to support her. Never once had Sarah had to question who or what she was. Looking in the mirror, her reflection never lied to her.

Leaning forward, she gathered herself and rested her arms on her legs. She needed something more. She demanded it, and every part of her yelled to settle down. Having never opened the closet door, she didn't know how to live there. It seemed so dark and alone, but if Karen was in there—she shook her head to make sure she knew it wasn't an option. There would be other women. In time, her heart could heal and she'd move on to someone who could hold her hand in public and say she loved her.

Her phone rang and she wiped at a tear she didn't even notice at first.

"Hello."

"Is this Sarah Lindstrom?"

"Yes, who's calling?"

"I'm a nurse in the ER at Regions in St. Paul. We have a woman here who listed you as her emergency contact in the past. She's currently unconscious, but we're going by her driver's license. Do you know a Lisa Anderson?"

"Lisa?" Sarah stood up as chills covered her body and her heart pounded in her head. "What happened?"

"She was involved in a car accident. I can't really go into more over the phone. Could you come to the hospital to help us with medical history?"

"Yes. I'll be right there."

"Before you go, do you know if she has any allergies?"

"No, none." Sarah hung up and turned to Mandy. "I have to go. Lisa's been in a car wreck."

"I'll go with you."

"No," Sarah spat, and then settled herself. "I can go by myself. It'll be fine."

"You're fresh off a break-up."

"Not really. I'm not anything."

"Then why are you rushing to your exes bedside?"

"She's my friend. Was for years. I'm still listed as her emergency contact. It must be from when I had to take her in for the flu. I don't know, either way her family is all from North Carolina. She needs someone there now."

"What about her new girlfriend?"

"What new girlfriend?"

"Exactly, you haven't spoken to her since February. You don't know what's going on in her life."

"When she wakes up she needs a familiar face. So what if it's me? She'll tell me if she wants someone else then."

"You want to hear that today? That even Lisa wants someone else?"

Sarah balled her fist and scrunched her face up. This was a stupid argument with a stupid person without the ability to make an attachment longer than thirty minutes. Before she said something she'd regret, Sarah turned and left.

The smell of harsh bleach chemicals assaulted her as she entered the Emergency Room. A short line was at the desk. She fidgeted with her keys as she stood. Her heart pounded at a pace she was unsure she'd be able to survive.

"Can I help you?" a nice woman in scrubs asked.

"Yes…I…um…my friend Lisa Anderson was brought in. They said I needed to come."

The woman typed on her screen, then wrote a room number on a visitor pass.

"Just head into the fourth room on the right."

"Thank you."

The doors opened and Sarah entered a bustling area where patients were being pushed from one room to another. A nurse was hanging a bag on an IV pole and smiled at Sarah. The last time she'd been here, Lisa was moaning like a baby after throwing up for a few hours.

When she entered the curtained area, she saw Lisa's dark hair now had hot pink streaks on the parts framing her face. She looked so peaceful laying there asleep even with the scratches and scrapes to her cheek bone and chin. Above her right eye was a gash being stitched by a doctor.

"Hello? Do you know our sleeping beauty?"

"Lisa, yes, we are friends."

"Good," he said. "She's got a pretty bad concussion. We've been able to rouse her a few times. You're not Sarah, are you?"

"Yes. Was she asking for me?"

"A few times." He tied off a suture, then snipped. "After we cast her leg she'll be admitted for observation. Luckily no surgery. The nurse will be in to ask some questions and I'm sure admitting, too."

The doctor stepped out and Sarah approached Lisa. Taking her delicate hand in hers Sarah leaned down and kissed Lisa's forehead.

"Hey lovely." She woke, but her eyes were heavy and barely opened. "You came." She swallowed hard. "How did you know?"

"You know how twins know when the other is hurt? It's the same with the woman I ask to marry me. For the rest of your life, I'll always know."

Lisa huffed a laugh with a small smile.

"At least until you change your emergency contact."

"Hmm...remind me when I'm not drugged and my brain isn't mush."

"I'll be your contact for the rest of your life with those parameters."

"Love you too, bitch."

"Rest Baby, I have to fill out your paperwork and you broke your leg so they have to set it."

"Will you give me my sponge baths?"

"You wish." Sarah kissed Lisa once more on her lips quickly and felt nothing.

How long had she felt that way? Even banged up and bruised Lisa was beautiful. The smell of her soap still lingered on her skin. Jesus, Sarah thought, she had no idea if Lisa was in a relationship. Worse yet, Lisa didn't even ask if Sarah had someone. Then again, she'd showed up when called. Just like their whole relationship.

Sarah updated all of Lisa's information the best she could and held her hand while they cast her leg. By the time she got to the room, Sarah hit the gift shop up for tabloid magazines, pop, and a half dozen snack items.

"I'm sorry," Sarah said as she stepped back out of view since a nurse was helping Lisa with a bedpan.

"Not like you haven't seen me with my ass half in the air before."

"It's a little different when someone's wiping it."

Michel Prince

"Jealous?" Lisa teased.

Sarah walked into the room and crossed her arms. The nurse was tucking her back into bed and arranging the blankets.

"Let me know if you need anything else," she said as she passed Lisa the remote.

"Drugs...copious amounts. Only slightly more than what is legal in Cambodia."

"I think you still have a *Tylenol* order I could give you."

"You're killing me."

"By the looks of it, I'm not the only one trying today." The nurse smiled as she passed Sarah.

"It looks like your boy crush got married this weekend." Sarah gave a fake pout and passed Lisa the magazine.

"That's why I crashed into a pole, the thought he and I would never make gorgeous swirl babies."

"Speaking of swirl babies," Sarah flopped in the recliner in the corner. "Gabbie's pregnant."

"Is she?" Lisa smiled. "I miss her. She's such a sweetheart. I thought Mandy was going to turn her at one point."

"Not enough alcohol I guess," Sarah said passively, as she popped a pretzel in her mouth.

"Aren't you glad I warned you the difference between a straight girl and a lesbian was six beers. Who knows who would have taken advantage of you and turned you to the dark side."

"That only works on the weak women." Sarah gave Lisa a little wink. "But thanks for the tip either way."

"How are the mafia members?"

"Status quo. Mary Beth is still the good little Catholic school girl."

"So sleeping with Eli, just not letting him spend the night?"

"Not when Luke's home." Sarah flipped through one of the magazines, not really looking at the bright fall fashions. "Mandy's...Mandy. She's a good roommate though."

"Just a roommate?"

"Yes." Sarah placed the magazine on her lap and looked at Lisa. "Although I might put a revolving door on her room just to save time."

"She came on to me you know?"

She didn't, Lisa did. Mandy had told her about the whole thing as a warning. At that time Sarah should have had torn loyalties, but she didn't. Mandy was who she sided with. Lisa never brought it up and Sarah had been too scared to be alone to call her on her bullshit.

"That's Mandy for you." Sarah snatched the remote and flipped through the channels.

"Hey, I'm injured."

"With a brain injury. Who knows what you'd choose. I'm not getting stuck watching pro bass fishing."

"One time," Lisa groaned. "I fell asleep. I swear I was watching porn and the DVD player turned off."

"Likely story."

"*Mr. Thompson, can you please speak on your policy concerning the global debt ceiling?*"

"You complained about bass fishing and you put it on a debate for student council."

"Actually," Sarah corrected. "It's for Congress."

"Since when do you know anything about politics?"

"I pay attention even when the amendment doesn't directly affect me."

"Sorry." Lisa moved her bed up and watched the comments. "What election is this for? You said Congress, but isn't the election in November?"

"The primary is next week. These are the Republican candidates for the Fourth District."

"You're not voting Republican, are you? They're against everything we believe."

"Lisa," Sarah snapped. "We're two different people. What you believe isn't necessarily what I believe. Not because I'm not as serious about lesbianism as you are, but because I have my own mind."

"Geez, fine. Didn't mean to offend." Lisa brushed back the hair that had fallen in her face and interrupted Karen's response. "I know I said some fucked up things to you the last time we were together. I was going to call and apologize, but…"

"My girls stopped you."

"Yes."

At one time the girls had tried to stop Case from seeing Gabbie. It didn't work because he was willing to fight for her. Even taking on the Growing Strong Mafia and all the dangers that entailed.

"Representative Schroeder, do not feign innocence. Your vote in support of the same sex marriage amendment flew in the face of all our party's policies. What excuse do you have for your vote?"

"She voted against her party," Lisa said with astonishment. "Wow, she's kinda cute in her power suit."

"Shut up," Sarah spat.

"I'm just sayin' her vote wasn't necessary to pass the bill. She could have abstained. Instead she took a stand. Maybe these jackasses have a few people with conviction."

"I want to hear her answer." Sarah stood and turned up the volume.

"I take you to a few protests and suddenly you're a poli-sci major."

Sarah glared at Lisa to shut her up, then returned to the screen. Karen clutched the podium in front of her. Even Sarah knew the answer to this question.

"There were other bills attached to the same sex marriage amendment, ones I did not want my supporters to think I forgot about. When in Congress I may have to compromise to get the bills I feel passionately about passed. We are a government that was built on the belief of working together and party politics allow the voters to know how you stand on issues. But the reality is in life we all concede at some point for the betterment of the whole." Etcetera etcetera.

But she didn't respond that way. She didn't respond at all, not even with a stock answer she'd rehearsed over and over.

"Representative?" the commentator prompted her. *"Did you need the question repeated?"*

"No, I just thought we weren't allowed to respond to each other's questions."

"Then let me ask you. Last year you voted against your party when it came to the same sex marriage amendment, what excuse do you have for this?"

"Can I ask for clarification? Are you asking for my reason for voting against my party? Because I've done that on a few other amendments." Her knuckles were white now from clutching the podium.

"Or are you asking why I voted for that amendment?"

Her head turned to her opponent.

"We both know which one we're all interested in." Walter Thompson leaned on the podium as if he had her. *"Why would you want a law that allowed gays to marry when our party sees it as an affront to the sanctity of marriage?"*

Over her opponent's shoulder Sarah saw the reporter from the softball game and she brought her hand to her mouth. Her stomach turned as she finally felt Karen's fear. Even with a level face, Sarah knew.

"Well," Karen swallowed hard, and then looked directly in the camera. For Sarah, she might as well of been talking directly to her. *"At the time of the vote I had no one in my life. I knew one day I'd find someone that I never wanted to let go of and I wanted the state and country I love to acknowledge our love was equal to my parents. They've been together for almost forty years and taught me a family comes from two people that love each other. Now I hope I can convince the woman I love to forgive me for being scared and marry me. And I'm proud that my one vote, even though it carried no real weight, is going to allow me the right if she accepts my proposal."*

"Representative, are you saying you are a lesbian?"

Karen bit at her bottom lip then straightened her shoulders. The auditorium was quiet, none of the murmuring that had accompanied the previous questions. The camera zoomed in on her and Sarah felt as if they were standing nose to nose. She could smell her perfume and taste her lips.

"Yes."

"And, uh," the moderator looked up from his notes, *"you're proposing to your girlfriend?"*

"If she'll have me."

Sarah tossed the remote on Lisa's bed.

"I have to go."

"You're abandoning me?"

"I was never really here. I'm sure you have someone else you can call."

"You're not..." Lisa pointed to the screen.

Sarah gave a sly smile and shrugged. "I guess I'm all that's needed to get a closeted Republican to come out."

* * * *

"Sorry you couldn't get the headline you wanted," Karen growled at Roger Porter, and then ran to Ashton's open arms.

He spun her around and for the first time she didn't feel like puking. Her head was light and so was her heart. No longer did she have the burden of hiding who she was and, for better or worse, such a public declaration meant she'd never be able to hide it again anyway.

When he put her down her feet found the floor and her hand found his out of habit.

"How could you?" her mother snarled, but Karen didn't flinch, not this time. "Why are you even holding his hand? Who is this woman you just proposed to on…nation… local TV? Thank God it's only local."

"It'll be on GMA, Today…all the national sites by tomorrow morning. I'm sure all the twenty-four hour networks will have it up in the next thirty minutes." Howard stormed in behind her mother. "We talked about this. Not now."

"You knew," her mother balked. "You didn't tell us. We could have gotten her help."

"Help for what, mom?" Karen asked. "What did I do wrong?"

"Do wrong? How could you lie with a woman? Ashton, what type of man are you that you just sat back and accepted it? Why didn't you show her how to behave properly?"

"What was he supposed to do? Tie me down and rape me?"

"Having sex with a man isn't rape."

"I need you to think about what you just said." Karen looked at her mother's enraged eyes. "Mom, I'm sorry I kept this from you for so long. Too long. But this is who I am. Who I have always been. I can't lie anymore."

"You're not my daughter. I can't even look at you." She turned and walked from the room, calling for her siblings to follow her. They did after giving Karen a sheepish shrug.

In politics, Karen had been slandered, muck racked, even had a little mud thrown her way. All of her choices, even the ones along the party lines, had been questioned at one time or another. Rejection came with her job, but not from her family. Maybe Darlene's acceptance had set her up for this failure. Because one family member hadn't burned her in effigy, she stupidly thought they'd all still embrace her. She waited for the weight of failure to replace the cloak of lies, but it didn't. Not this time. This time there was a chance Sarah would say yes and she'd have a new family. One that accepted her no matter how she voted or lived her life. They would be behind her even if her mother wasn't.

"I'm sorry sweetheart, but this is a little much for your mother," her father said. "And to do it publicly wasn't the way."

"I...didn't mean to..."

"You've placed us into a precarious position. You've taken away any option for us but to publicly accept your...choice. The voters might forgive this mess, but not being lied to." He turned to leave with the rest of her family, but stopped at the door. "I know you are good at being political, but I'm afraid you may have gone one step too far."

"What did I do, Ash?" she asked.

"Now you ask," Howard yelled. "Four more days. You couldn't wait four days for the primary."

"I've waited long enough. You've never noticed nor cared. Now you have a perfect reason to leave my campaign. No one will question it."

"Is that what you want, Peanut? Me to quit?"

"No."

"Good, because I can't quit you."

"Did he just go all Brokeback on me?" Karen asked Ashton.

"I think so...it's kinda weird." Ashton rocked his head from side to side like he was looking for something from Howard. "I thought his head was going to explode."

"It's his fault really, he wanted a proposal. You think she saw it?" Karen asked.

"Yes." Karen turned to see Sarah standing with her hand on the doorjamb. "To both questions. Unless you really did it just as some political stunt for Howard."

"I didn't," Karen replied as she tried to keep her eyes focused on Sarah. "I missed you."

"A friend was in the hospital, or I would have been in the audience."

"Really?"

"No."

"Can we get privacy?" Karen asked the people still milling around the room.

"Probably not here." Ashton pointed to the glass walls, and Karen sighed.

"I know a place." Sarah winked.

Ashton escorted the women out, only to get ridiculous questions. *"Are you a threesome? How long have you been sleeping together? Is this the woman, or are there more? Will you be getting married and having children? Will you adopt or use a donor?"* Karen had gone from stock political questions to paparazzi sex questions.

She should have felt like the walls were caving in on her, but instead she walked with a straight back and head held high. She was grounded. She no longer had to hide who she was.

Chapter Twelve

"Follow your inner moonlight; don't hide the madness."
—Allen Ginsberg

"I got her this time," Sarah said as she pulled Karen toward her car.

"You sure?" Ashton replied. "The reporter knows where you live."

"I have Mandy the attack dog at home."

"True."

They had barely made it two blocks before Sarah's phone went off.

"Yeah Mary Beth," Sarah answered with the phone on speaker.

"Turn on the news. You need to see this."

"I'm in the car." Sarah wove her fingers with Karen's. "Give me the play by play."

"Karen just asked to marry you. All the major news networks picked up the clip."

"I saw it live."

"You did? I thought you were at the hospital with Lisa."

"I was."

"So what are you going to do? She's out now! You can be with her. Are you going to?"

"What do you think I should do? I mean she's hot and all, but do I want to wake up next to the same woman for the rest of my life?"

"You're with her right now aren't you?"

"Yes."

"Okay, well tell her I'm sorry about her mom."

"What's wrong with your mom?" Sarah asked and squeezed Karen's hand.

"How did you know about my mom?"

"Oh…um…" Mary Beth stumbled. "They have audio of her saying you're not her daughter anymore."

"They have video, too?"

"A little, you were in a glass room."

"I'm so sorry, honey, I didn't know about that, she must have been the dark haired woman growling as I came in."

"I'd assume so," Karen sighed. "Thank you, Mary Beth, for the vote of confidence. I don't think I would have been strong enough if I hadn't met you and all your friends."

Mary Beth didn't respond. Sarah knew none of her friends understood how their strong friendship was seen to the outside world. It was a bond that most couldn't understand. They'd given up scholarships to support Mary Beth in her time of need. They rallied around Gabbie when her high school boyfriend screwed her over. Knowing the others were around with unconditional love every day had kept them all going at one time or another. Sarah had never questioned if her friends would accept her once she reached the age of dating. There was never a question.

"You're welcome," Mary Beth finally said. "I gotta go, Eli just got done tucking Luke in to bed."

The line went dead and another call came through from Gabbie. This time Sarah didn't play coy. She enjoyed that her friends were there for her and it made Karen relax and smile in a way she'd only seen in her bedroom before. Karen seemed to have so few times in life when she could be herself.

Entering her apartment, Sarah got the final supporter.

"Holy shit Sarah, you have to see this," Mandy called the moment the door was open. "Karen came out for you. I didn't think she had the balls."

"They're called ovaries. You have a pair, too," Karen teased. "Actually, Ash is afraid yours might be balls."

"Please say the gorilla isn't here."

"Not this time," Karen said.

"Well, I'm gonna crash at a friend's then, but just for tonight. I pay rent here, too."

"Yes ma'am," Sarah said with a slight nod.

Finally alone, they sat on the couch.

"This is the first time you've really sat out here with me," Sarah said as she pulled out Karen's French twist. Her auburn hair cascaded down to her shoulders and Sarah ran her fingers through it.

"The bedroom really killed two birds with one stone," Karen teased and moved closer. Her hand slid across Sarah's stomach, then traveled up her back. "I've so missed kissing you."

Karen's hand put the slightest amount of pressure and Sarah leaned in. The kiss was one she'd needed. Karen's lips were soft and glistened from the lipstick she wore. A hit of berry lingered on Sarah's tongue once she'd pushed past the lips.

Never had Sarah felt love exuded from a touch. Karen fell against her, but Sarah pushed back. Straddling Karen's hips her core burned in anticipation of making love to her. Karen's smell and essence ate away at Sarah's need to take her time. They had all night...no, they had the rest of their lives, but this moment she couldn't.

Karen had given up her whole life for Sarah. Suddenly Sarah's breath caught and she pulled back sharply.

"What?" Karen gasped with worry in her caramel eyes.

"You gave up everything. It just hit me."

"I don't know what or if I gave up anything. I'm still me. I'll still hold my office for another year. I'm still a politician, and I'm still who I've always been. Only now, thanks to you, I found the strength to let the people who voted for me know who I am. You helped me be an honest politician."

"Like I said, I ruined your career. Who would ever vote for that?"

"The last thing I want you to do is worry about me and my career. I'm fine."

"But—"

Karen captured Sarah's lips once more and brought her back to center. Her fingers curled around the hem of Sarah's shirt, pulling it over her head and tossing it to the side. Her hand, smooth with freshly manicured nails, scraped lightly against Sarah's back. Chills erupted along her spine and her nipples hardened.

Deftly, Karen unlatched Sarah's bra, and then slid her hands under the cups. She kneaded the swollen flesh while her tongue delved in Sarah's mouth. Trailing kisses from the side of her lips, to her chin, then neck, Sarah trembled. When Karen's lips came to Sarah's ear and whispered, the gentle breaths made her gasp. Her words made Sarah wet.

"Make love to me," Karen cooed.

Sarah sat back and removed her bra. Then climbed off of Karen only to help her stand up. Guiding Karen, Sarah turned her around. Brushing her hair to the side, Sarah lightly kissed her exposed neck.

A long zipper trailed down the back of Karen's business suit dress. The one piece, rather than two, allowed Sarah to slowly unzip and expose Karen's rose colored flesh. She kissed her way down until she could finally let the dress drop to the floor.

Standing in a bra, thong, and stockings, Sarah trembled at a vision she only imagined existed in one of Lisa's horrible pornos. Women didn't really dress this way. That was a lie, but here in front of Sarah stood Karen in matching red bra and panties. When she turned a little, only a triangular piece of lace stood between her and the sweet taste of Karen's flesh.

Sarah twisted her fingers around the thin band that hugged Karen's trim hips. Shimmying them down to the floor, Sarah worked her way back up with long licks and tiny bites.

The taste of arousal found her clutching Karen's ass as she laid a light kiss to her pussy before moving on. She didn't linger, not this time, although the desire was there. She wanted more, much more. Karen wanted to be made love to, and that couldn't be done with Sarah's head buried between her legs.

Karen's flat belly was Sarah's next stop as she rediscovered the woman she loved. It was as if every inch of skin were virgin territory. Untouched by her or anyone else. Karen's hand rested on Sarah's head until she found herself face to face with their bare chests caressing each other.

Taking her lips, she guided Karen to the floor as her fingers entered Karen's delicate folds. Wet and wanton, Sarah easily slid three, then four of her fingers inside while her thumb rubbed circles on Karen's clit. Slowly at first, Sarah found a rhythm that increased with her heartbeat.

"Look at me," Sarah commanded.

Their eyes locked for a moment until their lips could no longer hold back. Sarah's strokes increased and Karen clutched her back. Sarah's own core pulsed as the pleasure seemed to fall over her face like a waterfall. On the verge of her orgasm, Sarah felt truly connected, and the feeling sent both women into simultaneous moans and declarations of love.

Lost in the moment, Sarah was soon on her back with Karen tearing at her pants. Karen's fingers broke through the tightness caused by the shared release. The rush and penetration sent Sarah into another world.

Love. Ecstasy. Fear. Excitement. All of the emotions crashed in her mind and body as they both came, and then collapsed side by side.

* * * *

"I need to know. Why now?" Sarah asked, as she kissed the small of Karen's back.

They had eventually found their way to the bedroom. The night was coming to a close as the sun began peeking through the curtains.

"I'm tired, Sarah. If I go to sleep now, I can get thirty whole minutes before I'm due at the office. I told you last night anyway."

"I forgot it's Friday and we have to go back to the real world."

"Yes, we do, but thanks to you, I can actually go there with others knowing you love me."

"Fine, nap. I have the day off."

"Oh you bitch, no wonder you kept fucking me last night."

"Even if I had to work a double, I would have still fucked you all night."

Sarah kissed Karen and felt the tingle return between her legs.

"I'm going to have to drug you at night if I ever want sleep."

Somehow she must have fallen asleep because Karen woke with a kiss on her cheek, but she knew it wasn't Sarah. Ashton sat on the side of the bed with a to go cup of coffee. She had to start her day, but what day was it? She wondered how much of what she'd just experienced had been a dream.

Shifting her weight, she felt a cool breeze as the sheet fell and she knew it was all real. Naked in Sarah's bed she pulled the sheet to her chest and accepted the coffee.

"Morning, sunshine. You look worse than me. Did someone stay up past her bedtime?"

"Usually when I have to deal with your bullshit I've had two cups." Karen drank the warm brew with just the right amount of cream and sugar to make it tolerable. "Now," she sighed. "What do I need to know?"

"Did you turn on the TV last night?"

"No."

"Not even the Spice Channel? Playboy?"

Karen glared at Ashton.

"They probably would have had the coverage too anyway." He flipped on the small TV in Sarah's room and punched in the local news network.

It only took three minutes before the debate on her ability to be trusted came up. Then Walter's campaign ran an ad about her lying to not only her constituency, but her family as well. Who can Minnesotans trust in Washington?

She flopped back on the bed and pulled the pillow over her head.

"So, what's your plan? Howard wants a press conference by noon."

"Maybe my supporters didn't see it."

"We've lost three sponsors…but we found seven new ones."

"Really?" Karen popped back up.

"Lavender wants to interview you as well as three other magazines you may know."

"Because they are from the LGBT community."

"I assume so." Ashton passed Karen a croissant. "In the light of day, are you still happy you made the choice to come out?"

"Yes, but I haven't entered the real world yet."

"That's true. What about your mother?"

"I'm giving her a few days to calm down. I know Dar's got my back. Not sure about the rest of my sisters."

"Helen called to tell me how sorry she felt for me. All those years and what not, but I explained I knew. We talked for a bit. Alice and Rose checked in too, but only because they couldn't reach you."

"Maybe I didn't lose my whole family then."

"I doubt it. And you know your mom will come back if you win the primary."

"And if I don't?"

"Give her an extra week. You know she can't go a whole week without calling you about something."

"I hope so." Karen finished her coffee. "Any chance you have a change of clothes with you?"

"I'm nothing if not your humble servant."

"Thank you, I know you're probably getting some backlash."

"Nothing I can't handle. I've been around your rages. The shit I'm getting is child's play."

Dressed and ready to go, Karen found Sarah passed out on the couch. A few strands of her blonde hair fell over her cheek and Karen tucked it back. She stirred, but didn't wake.

"You really gonna marry her?" Ashton asked.

"Damn right I am. You gonna be my man of honor?"

"Me? Honor? I thought those two words were mutually exclusive." Ashton kept the quips coming the whole ride to work and helped Karen sharpen her orgasmically dulled senses.

The press was lined up outside Karen's office as they approached. Ashton kept one arm tightly around her and the other arm extended to keep them at bay.

"Representative. Representative," they called, but she kept moving with her head held high.

"Ashton, why are you still around?" One of them yelled.

"This is my office, where's yours?" he replied and pushed inside, then closed the door.

"Did you hear their questions?" Karen sneered. "Really? Am I going to step down?"

"Are you?" Howard asked as he shuffled papers on his desk. "Because I have two different statements for you to give. If that's an option I'll have to make up a third."

"No, it's not an option. I'm staying right where I am and proving my convictions are still strong."

"I like that." He said and scribbled something on a piece of paper. "Now I have two different releases. The first is if you wanted to say you were proving a point. You're not a lesbian. You love Ash…"

133

Karen glared at Howard who got the hint and crumpled up the piece of paper in his right hand. Ashton snatched it up and tossed it to the shred bin.

"Right, the other was you saying you still plan on running and being part of the RNC. I've contacted the head office and they want to talk to you before you meet the press at noon."

"The real world sucks." Karen took the press release and scanned it as she walked to her desk.

"I…um…have your…" Wendy, her secretary for the last two years, handed her a coffee mug. Her eyes were downturned.

"Thank you, Wendy." Karen took the mug. Wendy lingered. "Is there something else?"

"I am a trustworthy person." Wendy looked Karen in the eyes finally.

"That's good to know."

"And I've worked for a lot of different people. I don't judge."

"Wendy." Karen set the mug down. "The only people who knew before yesterday were Howard, who probably changed my diaper at one time in my life, and Ashton, who used to shove me in the lake when I was four. See the trend?"

"Lifetime friends."

"Yes. It wasn't personal. But I am happy that's why you're upset and not because of my choice of fiancé. Now if there is nothing else…"

"The Daughters of Snelling had a meeting with you at nine-thirty."

"Did they cancel?"

"No, but I'm assuming they aren't as understanding."

"We'll see in a half hour. Thank you."

Wendy left and Karen went back to reviewing Howard's speech. She scratched out the part about her making a choice. It had never been a choice. The only choice she'd made in her lifetime was to lie about it. That she put in bold letters and passed the speech back to Howard for revisions.

Ashton escorted the Daughters of Snelling representatives in and they sat on the couch. She and Ash took their usual spots in two wingback chairs.

"I'm so glad you came to meet with me today," she said. She knew the game, and although it had changed slightly, the pleasantries would be the same.

The two women looked at each other and despite how cordial they had been trained to be, they were anything but. Mrs. Paula Turner tightened her sweater over her chest as if Karen couldn't process with a pair of sixty year old breasts in front of her.

"We had approval from all our members to support you in your endeavor for a seat for the U.S. Congress." Her proper words were high pitched with just a hint of screecher howler monkey. "After your declaration last night we had to call a special vote."

"Nothing has changed in my politics. I've always voted with my conscience and heart. Most of those have stayed within the party lines."

"I don't understand how you can call yourself a respectable Republican," Mrs. Quinton Marshall bit.

"Mrs. Marshall, I hope your group will see my voting record and not my personal life."

"I understand in your generation you do not take personal improprieties as important, but we do."

"Improprieties are usually reserved for cheating spouses and child molesters. I am neither, but I appreciate you coming to tell me to my face that you will not be supporting my campaign and why."

"We didn't say that," Paula retorted. "Our membership voted to maintain our connection with your campaign. We've given your secretary our donation. We would ask that your...partner not be on stage with you, though."

"Is that contingent on your donation?"

"It's a suggestion. We've found people do not vote for alternative lifestyles and we hope you understand we are trying to back the stronger candidate."

"My partner will be at the rallies she has time to attend. I've hidden for over half my life. I don't want to hide anymore. I hope you can appreciate that."

"We cannot, but we are the minority in our group," Mrs. Marshall shuddered.

"Then why did you come instead of sending others."

"We are the chairwomen of the group. It is our duty. It's not the first time we had to deliver news that was opposite to our personal beliefs. One of the reasons we've stayed in our position is because we stand behind the majority."

"And the reason people have supported me is because my beliefs are out in the public for scrutiny. They know where I vote before I step on the floor. There was one part of my life that was hidden and that's no longer the case."

"Thank you ladies for coming today," Ashton said as he stood. "We appreciate your support."

"You," Paula glared. "You should be ashamed of yourself."

"Why is that?"

"How could you allow—"

"If your husband saw how hot her girlfriend is, he would have done the same thing."

"Ashton," Karen scolded as she held in a laugh.

"Why I never," Mrs. Marshall huffed.

"You should try it at least once in your life. Wait a second, didn't you go to an all girls school?"

The women left in a huff and Karen smacked Ashton upside his head.

"I thought you said you were handling the pressure?"

"I slipped. Sorry, no one attacks my Kare Bear." He bopped her nose with his finger. "No one but me."

Chapter Thirteen

"Love does not claim possession, but gives freedom."
—Rabindranath Tagore

"Asleep on the couch at one o'clock." Mandy's voice cut into Sarah's dream. "And dressed in only a camisole and a hot pair of panties."

Sarah whipped the blanket that had fallen to the side back over her butt, and then placed her hand on her ass to check the underwear situation.

"Let me get this straight," Sarah mumbled as she attempted to open her eyes, but failed. "Me in any pair of panties...granny or otherwise makes them hot?"

"Those weren't grannies, but I see your point. You waking up today?"

"Did you say it was one?"

"Yep."

"Ugh...let me sleep." Sarah pulled the cover over her face to hide from the day.

"Exactly how late did you stay up?"

"How do you do it?" Sarah asked from under the safety of her blanket.

"High protein diet, mandatory stretch breaks and B twelve."

"You're not funny."

"I'm the lonely single girl, what can I say? Always the bridesmaid. Speaking of which, tell me you didn't spend the night planning your wedding."

"Why?" Sarah snapped the cover back and sat up.

"Because you have time for that later. Last night was for funky monkey lovin'."

"You're scaring me."

"How?" she smiled. "I keep a list of how to freak you guys out."

"You've been against Karen since before I spoke to her, now suddenly you're gooey."

"Gooey. I'm never gooey. Sticky with a side of smacky-smacky, but never gooey."

"No." Sarah pointed as she looked at her friend. "Where did you sleep last night? You're happy."

"Am not. I'm fucking miserable. Day five million."

"You haven't been alive that long."

"You don't know how I was when I was just an egg. My mother's ovary sucks."

Sarah tried to read her friend, but couldn't. When Gabbie found Case, Mandy tail spun into depression. Then Mary Beth found out they were half sisters thanks to their father's wandering dick, and she'd been one level above Sylvia Plath.

"Are you on something?"

"Happiness for my friend, but that's wearing off."

"You're right. I shouldn't question. I'm glad, but I need to do one thing first."

"What's that?"

"Kill the told ya so fairy."

Sarah slapped the throw pillow across Mandy's face and she fell in mock death.

"Oh man it's one? I missed her press conference."

"Were you supposed to be there?"

"If I was, Ashton would have tossed me over his shoulder and carried me there, I assume."

"Let's pull it up. I'm sure it's online."

The girls grabbed Sarah's laptop and turned it on. While Mandy searched, Sarah found some pajama pants and they both flopped on the couch.

"You wanna read the comments first?"

"No, I might not want to do that at all. People feel strong when they have a computer in front of them."

"There might be good ones."

"You posted one, didn't you?"

"Maybe." Mandy quirked her head to the side. "Okay, so this is the one from her website."

Karen stood to the side of a podium with Ashton beside her. Should Sarah have been there? Maybe not yet. Not before the election. Now she became nervous as she saw Karen still held Ashton's hand.

Howard introduced her saying she would give a statement, and then answer questions after.

"Thank you all for coming." Karen began. *"First I'd like to apologize to my family and friends, whom I've kept the truth from for too long. Last night during the debate with Walter Thompson I revealed that I am a lesbian. Those who've spent the last year speculating on why I voted for the same sex marriage amendment got their answer. I've always voted my conscience and my conscience aligns with the Republican Party on the majority of issues. In fact, I've found I align more than most. Earlier today I spoke with the RNC about my choice to out myself during a debate. Although they supported my decision, they agree, as do I, that it was not the proper forum in which to make a public declaration of such magnitude."*

Karen took a sip of water. *"I am still the candidate backed by the RNC because, as I have said before, my politics and theirs align, and for that reason they will continue to support me as, I hope, will you. I do wish to publicly apologize at this time to my constituency for not being forthright on my preference. My friend Ashton Gilmore has stood by my side and helped in this deception."*

Karen turned her head and Ash nodded his approval. *"He is a true friend that knew at times people are not always willing to look past the first layer. His belief in me let me see that others can discover who I am and not run. As far as my partner, at this time I ask that you give her a small amount of privacy until she is brought up to speed with all that being in a public spotlight entails. I will take questions at this time."*

"Representative, who is the woman?" A male reporter asked.

"I will issue her name to the press at a later time."

"Is she also in the closet?" A different voice called.

"No, but I'm a public figure, she is not."

"Did she accept?" A female reporter queried.

"My proposal? Yes."

"Representative, how can the citizens of your district trust you when you hid and lied about such a major part of who you are?" Another female asked.

"Our sexuality is a major part of who we are as people," Karen took a long cleansing breath. *"But even the citizens of my district don't want every part of their life on display for the world to see. I hope they understand I wasn't trying to deceive them, I just had a part of who I was that I wasn't ready to share."*

"What about your mother?" A male reporter called. *"Have you spoken to her since last night?"*

"No, I'm giving her time to absorb what I revealed. I've known since high school who I'm attracted to, but I've been too scared to share it with my family. A few members of my staff knew, but aside from that I hadn't shared. This was my mistake and why I apologized to my family. I shouldn't have said what I said in an open forum and not during a debate where the issues affecting the citizens of Minnesota were supposed to be discussed. It was a time for voters to see where Walter Thompson and I stand on the issues that matter to them the most."

"Is this just a stunt to pull in last minute voters?" A man asked.

"I've lost and gained supporters in the last twelve hours. I've discovered who my friends are and saw some walk away. I can't even qualify your question with an answer because it doesn't deserve one."

"Where is this mystery woman, or are you still trying to produce one?"

"She exists and will be introduced at a later time."

"If she's out, why is there a problem?"

"I'm not protecting her from the world finding out she's a lesbian. I'm protecting her from reporters who cross lines when it comes to personal privacy."

Karen looked at one reporter, but Sarah couldn't make out which one. Snapping shut the laptop, she sighed.

"I should call her."

"Yeah, did she give you her real number?"

"We were kinda preoccupied."

Sarah went to her room and found her phone. Hopefully Howard gave Karen back her throw away phone. After two rings, she found out.

"I miss you so much."

"I slept through your press conference, but I watched most of it on the computer."

"How far did you get?"

"The accusation that I'm imaginary."

"That was original. I didn't expect that."

"You could have used my name."

"I didn't even think about it until I saw Howard put it in the speech. Ashton asked if I was sure you'd be okay with it. I tried to call, but—"

"I was passed out in the other room."

"I wish I could do the same. I'm getting a headache from lack of sleep."

"I'm sorry, honey. Do you have any time to rest?"

"Yes, before a dinner tonight."

"You have a date, or is it too soon?"

"Let me check if I can get an extra seat. I'd love to take you, but know Ashton will probably be there, too."

"What's a date without Ash?"

"A night of uninterrupted seee…I gotta go. Call you later."

"You were going to say sex, weren't you?" Sarah teased.

"Yes."

"And you got caught?"

"Ash is here."

"Give him kisses from me."

"I doubt he wants that. I'll call you back, love you."

"Love you, too."

Sarah walked back to where Mandy was and looked at her.

"What does one wear to a rubber chicken Republican dinner?"

* * * *

"It's too soon," Howard snapped. "It's three days until the primary."

141

"And I'm already being accused of pulling a stunt and creating a girlfriend."

"This group is close to canceling their sponsorship. You need their vote. It's a large company with thousands of workers who tend to vote the way the boss does."

"Howard—"

"Karen, listen to me."

"I have, for years. This morning the Daughters of Snelling dropped off a check because against the judgment of their chairwomen, the members still voted to keep supporting me. I grew up in this town. People know me."

"They thought they knew you. Thought. This is what you don't understand."

"I understand it."

"You might get past old Walt, but I don't think you can beat Barbara now."

"Then I won't. Howard, I'm happy being in the State House. You want more."

"Don't delude yourself now that you're all ready to get married."

"I'm not. Someday maybe I'll go to Washington. Hopefully in January, but if not—"

"If you're not a hundred percent committed to this, then drop out."

"I am, but Howard—"

Ashton came in the room and turned on the TV. Astrid's face was dead center. She had her hand up trying to block the camera.

"Are you the girlfriend Representative Schroeder proposed to last night?"

"No. Why are you following me?" Astrid cried.

"You are one of her former lovers are you not?"

"I worked on her campaign a few years ago. That's it."

"Turn it off."

"Are you sure?" Ashton asked.

"Astrid wasn't even a hundred percent sure she was gay. That's why she was perfect for me. She didn't want to come out in any way, shape, or form. She's getting married to a man in two months. I was the only woman she'd been with."

Karen pinched the bridge of her nose. Astrid didn't deserve this. Who knows if they'd already found Vonnie.

"Sarah's coming with me to the dinner. I'm ending this before Vonnie loses her daughter. Her ex looks for any reason to prove she's an unfit mother."

"I'm still against it," Howard warned.

"Noted. Now call and say I'll need an extra plate."

"Why?" Ash asked.

"I still need you by my side. You're one of my assistants and damn it, you're my friend."

"It'll be okay," Ash replied.

"Of course it will." Karen flopped back in her chair.

Three hours later, Karen was at home flipping through her closet, looking for the right outfit. There really wasn't much choice. Power red for the hundredth day.

"Why don't I wear green more often?"

"It is a tranquil color. Maybe you just like getting everyone's heart pumping," Ashton replied from his closet. "I'm going to have to move my stuff out soon huh?"

"Eventually, yes."

"Down the hall to the guest room, or all the way home?"

"Home. Something tells me last minute outfit changes won't be happening."

"How did Sarah take the news when you told her it was a formal event?" Ashton walked into Karen's closet while attaching his cufflinks.

"I didn't know panic could be conveyed so easily over the phone. Luckily she had a few hours to prepare."

"Did you tell her what color your dress was? I'd hate to think of you two clashing."

"We're lesbians. It's expected," Karen teased.

"I'm really proud of you, Kare Bear. I don't think I've told you that yet, but what you did took guts."

"It was overdue."

"I don't think so. You've only known her for a month. Asking her to marry you took balls."

"They're called ovaries." Karen tossed a shoe at him.

143

"And the other thing. You look amazing now."

"Before, what was I?"

"A cute chick that had a huge burden on her shoulders." He cupped her cheek and kissed her forehead. "It showed."

Karen waited with Ashton outside the venue for Sarah to arrive. When she did, the vision of her caused Karen to catch her breath. A slick, gold, satin dress hugged her curves. The plunging neckline accentuated her breasts, which weren't held back by a bra. They couldn't be, the V of the neck landed between them. The dress went to her ankles where she attempted to walk in lower heels. She reached back in her car for a half coat with long sleeves and a sensible, conservative collar.

"Too much?" she asked with her hands upturned. In the right one was her clutch.

"Yes, you have way too much covering that body of yours."

She smirked.

"You don't clash," Ashton said. "In fact, you look perfect together."

Karen extended her hand and Sarah entwined her fingers with Karen's. Not roughly, just right. Soft and delicate. Karen knew she'd have a hundred sweaty, hard handshakes for the next hour or so—the reprieve of a few moments with Sarah gave her hope for the future.

The reporters were in the lobby of the St. Paul Hotel where the dinner was being held. They rushed as if a starter's pistol had been squeezed off. Sarah curled tighter to Karen and held on to her bicep.

"Representative, is this your fiancé?"

"Yes, this is Sarah Lindstrom."

"Where's the ring" Another reporter asked.

"Thanks for calling me out on being a cheapskate."

"How long have you two been an item?"

"Long enough to know I don't want to spend another moment without her," Karen said.

"Sarah," A TV reporter asked, and Sarah turned, only to be blinded by the light above the camera.

"Sorry." She waved her hand as her beautiful, blue eyes squinted. "Can I help you?"

"Sarah, who are you?"

"I'm…a teacher and business owner."

"Were you surprised when Representative Schroeder asked to marry you?"

"Yes and no."

"We need to get in to dinner." Ashton came to the rescue and ushered the women past the reporters.

"Now I see why you keep Ash around."

"Yep," he teased. "I'm the real muscle in Team Schroeder."

"We need to come up with a signal," Sarah suggested.

"A signal for what?"

"If I'm doing something wrong. Like tug your ear or squeeze my hand."

Karen brought her finger under Sarah's chin and lifted it up.

"You can't do anything wrong. You're me and I'm you." She laid a light peck on Sarah's lips, and then heard cameras going off. "Really? When was the last time you took a picture of a politician kissing their spouse?"

"They do it all the time," Ashton grumbled into her ear. "Quit being so sensitive."

Karen turned to Ashton and sighed. "Protect her, even from me."

"Gotcha, boss lady."

"Representative Schroeder, I'm Sherman Jensen." A portly man approached and shook Karen's hand. "It's so good to have you here tonight."

The tight squeeze and clammy palm instantly repulsed her. She no longer knew what she was doing here. Why couldn't she just curl up and live in Sarah's apartment. Or have her move into her home? Why did she want to be a politician? It's a nasty chess game she still hadn't mastered. Her every move was questioned. She had ideas, but was too young to get the backing in the State House. The only power she really had was her vote.

"I'm happy to have your support."

"Hey." He nudged her, and she wondered how red a face could be before it exploded. "I got a second cousin that's gay. No reason to judge here. Plus, it looks like you've got a real classy lady there."

If he made one comment about a better half, she may have to use the one free pass Ashton gave her to have him kill someone. Even if he was kidding, she still thought he may cash it in for her.

"It's a good thing you came out instead of being exposed. How close was the reporter with the story?"

"I have no idea what you're talking about."

"There was a reporter, right?" Karen's skin began to crawl. "That's why we all clean out skeletons, no reason to be caught in a lie."

"There wasn't a reporter. I came out because the time was right."

"Okay, well, Representative, we have made an extra space at the head table."

"Thank you. Is there a place where I can get a breather?"

"Oh…oh yes. We have a room upstairs where there was some staging things set up. If you'd like I can give you the key."

"I'd appreciate it." Karen tugged on Sarah's hand and Ashton also followed suit. "I need to get out of here."

Chapter Fourteen

"If you cannot inspire a woman with love of you, fill her above the brim with love of herself; all that runs over will be yours."
—*Charles Caleb Colton*

"For those just joining us, we're about to see a level four melt down," Ashton commentated as if he were a sportscaster. "Which is a good thing because I'm sure the rookie, Sarah Lindstrom, has yet to witness this side of the walking disaster she's about to marry."

"Fuck off," Karen growled right before she stepped off the elevator toward the staging room. Opening the door slowly she made sure no others were around and the door was closed before she let out a howl.

"Does this happen a lot?" Sarah asked Ashton as Karen grabbed a pillow and began to pummel it repeatedly.

"Be glad we're not at her house. Her mother is still wondering what happened to the vase she gave her as a house warming gift."

"I'm in the room. I'm a damn person. I can hear you."

"This is stage two, I'm impressed. Rarely does she have this much control."

"Did you hear that asshat? Seriously, I have a third cousin twice removed that knew a lesbian."

"Her quoting ability loses its accuracy around..." A pillow flew through the air and smacked Ashton right in his face. "Stage three. Sadly, her throwing arm does not."

"Karen, honey, why are you so mad?"

"Why am I so mad? Why am I so mad?" The last mad came out slightly below the pitch only dogs can hear. "Why are they acting this way? It doesn't make sense? It's not the sixties. It's not the eighties. Jesus, rappers can be gay, but I can't?"

"It's not that you can't," Sarah said as she walked across the room and risked her life by clutching Karen's hand. Not squeezing, she chose to be delicate to remind her most of the world wouldn't be that way. "It doesn't matter what the relationship is that you're in, if you deviate one step from the norm, people will say different things. One of my best friends is married to a black man, the other is dating a Hispanic guy. You think they don't get comments or looks?"

"No, I don't."

Sarah led Karen to the bed and sat her down.

"When I was up at the capitol protesting, an older couple came up to me. She was white and her husband black. They must have been in their early seventies. After thanking them for showing their support I asked them why they chose to stand with us that day." Sarah smoothed back a piece of Karen's hair that had fallen from its binding. "When they got married it was illegal in most of the country. Alabama didn't lift their ban officially on interracial marriage until two thousand and ten. Gabbie and Case get comments all the time. It's become a joke between just them. People don't even realize how hurtful or stupid they sound."

"I can't even understand why this is making me so mad."

"Me either? Did you think they were going to throw you a ticker tape parade?"

"Part of me thought it would be fine. Everyone would be like, oh…that's why Ashton never married her and why it was okay he was a slut with half the women on her staff."

"According to the news, so were you," Ashton teased, only to get another pillow smacked at his groin this time. Sarah didn't even know where it came from.

"Karen, let's make their comments be a joke between us. It's easy to do and it will help you wind down. The important thing is that these people still want to support you. You've said it a dozen times now, your politics haven't changed. You'll vote the way you always have and that's what you care about. If people support you just because you're gay, they're as dumb as the people that don't because you are."

Karen rubbed the bridge of her nose, and then stood up. Locating the pillows used as weaponry, she made the room look as if she'd never been there.

"Thank you, Sarah." Karen extended her hand and Sarah got up, giving Karen a little kiss when she did.

"For someone in politics, you need a thicker skin."

"Ninety eight percent of the world can go by me and spit on my shoes with no effect."

"That's a good percentage. I'll be there for the other two."

At least with this girlfriend she had Ashton as back-up. Something was bothering her, though. Why should she be a mother to the woman she loved? It was an ugly side of Karen, and if it continued she wasn't sure if she could step back into that role again.

During dinner, Sarah tried to listen and focus on what was going on. Instead she was mulling over the past twenty-four hours. She had rushed to the hospital to care for Lisa who had turned out to be the bitch she always knew she was. What had she been thinking? Taking care of that walking disaster…walking disaster, those were Ashton's words.

She looked at Ashton who sat with a smirk on his face as Karen made a few jokes written by others. Sarah didn't want to walk away like Mandy did when the person made one mistake, but she also didn't want to be Mary Beth, hanging on for years for the dream of what might be.

After dinner Karen was talking with a few people when Ashton placed a penny in Sarah's hand. She looked at it, then him.

"Now you have to tell me what's kept you from the thrilling discussions tonight."

"I don't understand."

"I gave you a penny, now why are you a thousand miles away? I know the difference between zoning out and lost in thought." Ashton leaned against the wall. "You've been funky since we came down. Have you never seen someone spaz out before?"

"What you rank level three barely registers with my friends. Gabbie believes the stress ball we gave her was meant for whipping at the head of the person ticking you off."

"Then what?"

"I really shouldn't—"

149

"Karen's my best friend, but it doesn't mean I tell her everything I hear. If I did she'd have known Roger Porter was getting really close. I keep things from her when I know there's nothing she can do about it or she'll overreact."

"How often do you talk to her?" Sarah joked.

"Not as often as I should."

"It's just I've always been a caretaker for my girlfriends. That's not been successful."

"Devil's advocate?"

"Sure."

"Karen has never been one to be taken care of. It seems that way, but nothing I say or do would alter the way she was already going. In the room upstairs you cut out about ten minutes of her breaking down, but if you weren't there, she'd have had her hissy fit then come back down and be the smiling woman you see over there."

Ashton pointed. Karen was holding the hand of a board member and laughing as she wished them goodbye.

"You're in a very small circle that gets to see the real Karen. Sadly, as truthful as she's being with these people, she's human, and the reason she became a politician was to change the world. Corny as it sounds, she actually cares about the environment, taxes, the poor, and for some reason, small dogs."

"Just the small ones?"

"No, but I jump when a dog barks and his voice is lower than mine."

"Ash." Sarah took his hand and squeezed.

"Yeah."

"You're not bad for a gorilla."

"Can I come over just to piss off Mandy tonight? The reunion show is on for The Peach Tree Wives."

"And you have a death wish."

"Gotta get your jollies where you can."

* * * *

On the morning of the primary Karen rolled over, kissed Sarah, and then did what she did every election—waited for a call from her mother. They usually woke her between five and six in the morning. When her clock clicked to six she stared at the ceiling and pulled Sarah in tighter. She had her leg wrapped around Karen's and her head on Karen's chest. Her arm returned the hug as she begged for five more minutes.

In two hours the polls would open, and Karen would go to her polling station and vote. She never thought about Sarah and if she voted. It was assumed she would, but then again it was the primaries and Sarah might not be registered with the Republican Party. Her morning was already off. She should be in the shower by now, but without her mother's call, she couldn't move.

At six fifteen she needed to at least let Sarah get going to work. When her phone rang, Karen breathed a sigh of relief.

"Hey Kare Bear," Ashton cooed. Karen couldn't speak. Her mother had actually disowned her. "Karen."

Karen untangled from Sarah and went into the bathroom.

"Yes, sorry, do I have anything but the vote today?"

"You have one meeting at ten about the reservoir. Then a night counting votes at the election office."

"Fun, have you put in the pizza and pop order?"

"Done. I'll see you at the polling place?"

"Yes, let me hop—" Karen's phone beeped and she pulled it away from her face to see her mother calling. "I have to go. Mom's on the other line."

"Love you, lady."

"Love you, too." Karen clicked over. "Hello, mom?"

"I hope you're not running late this morning. My alarm just hasn't had the same effect on me since your father retired."

"I'm up. You know Ash has your back."

"Yes, I guess he would." Her mother sighed. "Karen, I've been praying about your situation."

Karen made a fist and added the comment to the Sarah funny shit bank they'd created.

"Pastor Winston helped me understand it wasn't your choice to go against God."

"Is that a direct quote?" If it was, the bank may overflow.

"Not exactly, but...I...you're still my daughter. And if this woman you've found makes you happy, I need to accept that fact."

151

"Are you ready to meet her?"

"No." her mother swallowed hard. "And I'm not a hundred percent with this whole change in you, but I'm still going to vote for you. I just thought you should know I believe you are the right person for the job no matter what happens in your off hours."

Sarah walked in and wrapped her arms around Karen's belly as she rested her head on her shoulder.

"Thank you. I do hope you change your mind about the other thing. Sarah's mother is throwing us an engagement party in a few weeks. You should be getting an invitation soon."

"Sarah, that's her name?"

"Yes, Sarah Lindstrom."

"Is she taking your name?"

"We haven't gotten that far, but I'd assume we'd keep our own names."

"This is all too much for me right now. I'll call you after the poll numbers come in."

"I look forward to it."

"Have a good day, Karen."

"Love you, mom." The line went dead.

"You okay?" Sarah asked as she kissed Karen's neck.

"Ask me after results are in."

"You want breakfast?"

"I don't eat on election day. My belly can't handle it."

"Okay, but a big celebration dinner tonight, right?"

"Yes."

Sarah climbed into the shower, and then poked her head out giving Karen a come hither look. "Hey Representative, what's your stance on water conservation?"

* * * *

"If you're moving out I need to know sooner rather than later," Mandy said as Sarah entered her classroom.

"Don't you have to be in the Children's House area?"

"Don't you need to let a girl know if you're not coming home?"

"This from you?"

152

"Fine, it's just I can't afford your rent."

"I'm up for renewal in October. I'll talk with Karen, but I'm pretty sure I'll move in with her by then. I'm not sure. Let's get through the election. For all I know she may end up in Washington for half the year. One step at a time."

"I need to know by the end of the week if I need to find a new home."

"Deal."

"Why do I even throw away moving boxes?"

"Have you considered buying a house?"

"I can't afford an apartment."

"Talk to Eli, I think you'd be surprised."

"Let me add that to my list of things to do today…win the lottery."

The kids were slowly finding their way to the room. Soon Sarah could be in her own classroom instead of what was considered their daycare center. The final walkthrough was later today with the contractors to make sure everything was good and safe. Most of the kids just wanted to play in the gym, especially on an overcast day that foretold a pending storm this afternoon.

"I actually got through fifteen minutes on the local news without hearing your name," Mary Beth said as she came through the door.

"On election day, not good."

"It was. Karen had been interviewed last night after an event and there you were, the dutiful wife."

"Those events are cutting into my sleep." Sarah yawned. "I'll be happy when it's over."

"It's just getting started if she wins."

"I should have a serious discussion about running for Senate so we don't have to do this every other year."

"You think she'll win?"

"Today yes."

"Not in November?" Mary Beth asked as she sat in one of the small children's chairs. Her long legs, which had been such an attractant to Eli, bent past her chest because of the low seat.

"Right now she's kinda of in a bad place. She's happy to be with me, but I can see regret. I'm not sure what it's about, though. Karen's successful. Always has been. This is her first taste of real failure."

"She never lost a race?"

"A few in college, but who actually pays attention to campus politics? Promise energy drinks in the quad and suddenly you're a forward thinker."

"I wouldn't know," Mary Beth replied. "Are you ready for all this?"

"Honestly, no," Sarah admitted. "I love Karen. I just wish we would have met after her last election so I could ramp up to this."

"Look at it from a psychological standpoint."

"Oh dear lord, why are you in school?"

"A middle child who finally gets attention."

"I'm sure you had a real reason for coming in here this morning."

"I do. Your popularity is having a strange effect on our enrollment."

"How?"

"An increase. We have ten new families that want to do a walkthrough over the next two days. I was thinking of staying late one night for one more open house."

"We already have the welcome to school night."

"I know, but the potential of ten new families…maybe even more."

"Why do they want to come? To ogle me? Because I'm a lesbian and they want their children taught by one? I'm not a novelty."

"People know the name of our school now. Feel the parents out, then let me know."

The time had come for Sarah to be insulted.

"Feel them out?" Her voice had a methodical, slow tone to it.

"Did I say something wrong?"

"Why am I supposed to feel them out?" Sarah straightened out a domestic learning tool. "Is that my job now?"

"Hold on, you were the one who said she didn't want to be the token lesbian. How would I know if they want to be at the school to watch you or educate their children?"

"I'm sorry, my nerves are a little raw right now. I've had more snide comments in the last few days then I've had in my whole life. I didn't come out of the closet, I was born on the outside. When I had a girlfriend no one looked at me twice. I have had to spend so much time keeping Karen calm, I haven't had time to comprehend everything."

"Entering a relationship is scary. I couldn't imagine being in a public one. I get enough scrutiny from Luke's dad." Mary Beth took Sarah's hand in hers. "Mandy and I will handle the new parents. You know she can sniff out anyone's motives. Go celebrate with your girl."

"Ms. Sarah," Theo said as she tugged on her shirt.

"Yes Theo."

"My mommy says you're getting married."

"I was asked, but it will be a while before I get married."

"Oh, can I come?"

"I don't **know**, do you think you'd want to come to my wedding?"

"Yes."

"Well, when it gets closer we'll talk more about it."

"Okay, my mommy says you're marrying a pretty lady."

"Tell your mother thank you."

Theo took off in search of a friend and Sarah dropped her head in her hands.

"Just two days ago I was chastising Karen for being too sensitive, now here I am ready to snap on everyone."

"You want my two cents?"

"What is it with people giving me pennies?" She waved off Mary Beth's confused look. "Yes, what would you like to add?"

"This is the first time you met someone on your level."

"Karen's amazing, she's done so much—"

"You both bring things to the relationship at an equal level...does that make sense? There was a lot of hand holding with your previous partners. Not with Karen, or at least it's the same amount."

"Are we rushing?"

"A few years ago I'd of said yes, but after Gabbie and Case I learned the speed of falling in love is individual."

"Eli hasn't asked you yet, has he?"

"I scare him and I have a kid. Plus, I'm not the hopeless romantic the rest of you are."

"Since we have the same dad, is it nature or nurture?" Mandy asked as she joined the conversation.

A handful of kids came through the door, allowing Sarah to table the discussion. Today was about Karen and that was going to be her only focus…that and Theo, who decided to use the counting rods as a ninja sword.

Chapter Fifteen

"If you're going to kick authority in the teeth,
you might as well use two feet."
—*Keith Richards*

"How soon until you're here?" Karen asked Sarah as she stared at the early numbers.

"I have to stop and vote, and then I'll be there. How many times can I do that? Is it like American Idol, just in person?"

"Please say you're joking." Karen rubbed her stiff neck. The ramifications of this vote weighed heavily upon her.

She knew in theory her mother would eventually accept her and Sarah, but the idea had been planted that she needed to win this election. Suddenly it was more than an election—it had become the culmination of her life. Jesus, she was being dramatic.

"Would you like me to pick up anything on my way there?"

"No, I told you I don't eat on election days."

"Wait…this may be a problem because I expected some celebratory sex when you win."

"What if I lose?" Karen laughed.

"Then you should expect some consoling sex."

"My evening's planned. Why am I hanging out here?"

"I have no clue. Now let me find my fake ID's so I can vote for you ten times on my way over there."

"Sarah?" Karen said as she cupped the end of the phone. "I love you."

"Love you too, see you in…what the hell?"

"What happened?" Karen gasped.

"Since when do people vote in a primary during mid-terms? The line is insane."

"You've been around me too much. You sound like a politician."

"Is it getting you wet? Come on…you can tell me. You know it is. Trust me, I know the feeling. Just admit it. If I go into a dialogue about corporate bailouts crippling the social security system, you'll find a way to reach through the phone to make out with me."

"There is a chance." Howard poked his head around the corner and waved for her to come. "I have to go, see you in a little bit, love you."

"Love you, too."

"What's up?" Karen asked as she rounded the corner.

"Early numbers are coming in."

"They've been coming in."

"You're ahead sixty-three percent to thirty-four."

"That doesn't equal a hundred."

"There's a plus or minus of two for error."

"Still not a hundred," Ashton said as he took a bite of pizza and hopped on a desk. "Remember I did pass math."

"Why do you act like this is your first election every time?" Howard growled.

"Because it's the one time a year we can get over on you." Karen smiled. "Where's the reporting at?"

"Three percent."

"I will never understand how with such a small percentage you can claim me the victor."

"Did I say victor? Or did I say winning?"

"Fucking politicians," Karen grumbled as the clock ticked off another second.

"Hey lady," Ashton called as he wiped off his fingers. There was an unnatural way he could devour a piece of pizza in less than five seconds. "When's your lady love coming?"

"After she votes. She says the line's pretty long at the polling place."

"In that case how about playing hooky with me for a few minutes?"

Karen looked around her campaign headquarters and saw the drag of the mid hours. Last minute campaigning ended around three. Now they were in vote tallying time, but that really didn't count until at least eight. If she stayed here, she'd be stuck watching Ashton, the human vacuum, eat an entire pizza, and Howard would bug her with every update.

"I'm all yours."

They left the office and Karen breathed in deeply to capture the fresh air. Sadly, the office was on a busy street. It was as loud outside as in. Wasn't playing hooky supposed to be fun? Ashton opened his passenger door and Karen got in. They drove for about five minutes until he pulled up in front of a jewelry store.

"Now I was raised to know that when you ask a woman to marry you, it includes a ring."

"I'm not sure that's how it works for Sarah and I."

"Why? The bands are there as a sign of fidelity...hence why even when I faked being the love of your life, I never let you put on a ring."

"A ring should be bought after long thought and...I don't know. I can't just pick any ring," Karen said.

Ashton got out and walked toward the store. Karen hopped out of the car and called after him, "Ash, come on."

"What's it going to hurt to look?"

"I just got my lesbian card punched. If I go in there, I'm liable to have it taken away."

"Do you even believe what you're saying?"

"No, but I'm looking for a good stalling tactic."

"Why?" Ashton asked as he held open the door. "Because it'll be real if you put a ring on her finger?"

Karen balanced herself on the car door, rocking herself back and forth on her heels. Ashton raised an eyebrow at her, and she caved.

"Ten minutes, that's it." She rushed in behind him and they were greeted by a salesman the moment they entered.

"Who's scared to put a ring on?" he smiled with is hands together.

"My buddy here asked her girlfriend to—"

"Aren't you running for Congress?" the man asked.

"Yes, yes I am," Karen said as she extended her hand out of habit to shake. "I'm Representative Karen Schroeder."

"You're not in my district sadly, but I did see your press

conference." He walked toward a display case. "We have a lovely selection in bridal jewelry."

Diamonds sparkled in a case in every size and cut. Gold, platinum, and even titanium bands held the jewels tightly. Karen placed her hands on the metal part of the case to avoid smudging the glass. She felt like a five year-old at Candyland downtown. So many delicious choices.

Scanning from left to right she became overwhelmed. Stepping back, she closed her eyes and looked once more. Then she walked along the case. Tucked toward the back, a ring caught her eye.

"That one," she whispered as if declaring it out loud could make it disappear.

The salesman pulled the ring from the case and placed it on a small, soft cloth. The titanium band did not go all the way around, instead it was linked by the emerald cut diamond in the center. The matching wedding band was lined with emerald cut inset baguettes circling the band. It was perfect.

"Thank you, Ash," Karen said on the ride back.

"I'm your wingman, it's my job."

Sarah's car was in the parking lot when they pulled up. The ring sizing took longer than she'd thought. Luckily the store's jeweler hadn't left for the day and the adjustment was able to be done that night. Karen tucked the wedding band into her purse, but she held the engagement ring box in her hand. The smooth velvet caressed the inside of her palm as she tried to tuck it to the side.

When they walked through the door, Sarah's lips curled up even though she'd just taken a big bite of pizza. Placing the rest of the slice on a paper plate she covered her lips. With sparkling, blue eyes smiling at her, Karen crossed the difference between them in no time to sit on the edge of the desk where Sarah had set up camp.

"You made it."

"Barely," she sighed after she swallowed. "You're lucky I love you because there was a line outside of the polling place."

"Were they giving cookies away? That always draws a crowd."

"I wish." Sarah looked at the pizza, then back at Karen. "Any chance you'll be ordering more pizza?"

"We have the Savoy on a schedule. Every two hours until ten they drop off a dozen pies."

"Thank God." Sarah took another bite. "I had to wrestle a volunteer for this. Don't be mad, but I pulled rank."

"Does this mean she out ranks me?" Ashton asked.

Karen sat back and looked at the two most important people in her life and smiled. "Maybe, I think a Mario Kart race will be in your future to determine dominance."

Ash picked up a remote and turned up the volume as numbers rolled in again. Sarah got up and stood behind Karen. Her hands rested at first on Karen's shoulders, but Karen needed more. Her arm reached around and she placed her hand on Sarah's back. Pulling her close, Sarah easily curled her arms around Karen's body.

"You're doing well, Karen."

"For now, seven percent reporting. It's just exit polls."

"You're up by double digits."

"I'm nervous."

"About what?"

"People saying they voted for me to be PC."

"They're not being filmed, hun, I'd understand if they were."

"I'm in a weird place."

"Why?"

"I don't want people to vote for or against me because I came out." Karen rubbed the velvet box still in her hand behind Sarah's back.

"Get over it. I don't care why they vote, as long as you win."

Karen turned her head and was nose to nose with Sarah. With a light kiss she brought her hand to right under Sarah's nose.

"Wh...wha...what is that?"

"I don't know? Guess you'll have to open the box and see."

Sarah held the small, white, velvet box in her hand. Her thumb smoothed out the grain. A tear could be seen on the corner of her eye. The creak of the hinge on the box made Karen's heart race. Sarah gasped and snapped the box shut.

"That is beautiful."

"It reminded me of you. Strong, lightweight, and sparkles in any light."

Sarah opened the box once more. Her hand trembled as she tried to

161

put the ring on. Karen took the small piece of metal and slid it on Sarah's third finger. Sarah's hands cradled Karen's face as she kissed her. When they broke from the embrace she noticed the loud room had silenced. Her face reddened, then she leaned in and gave one more small kiss.

"Walter's on the phone," Howard said as he placed his hand on Karen's shoulder.

"What does he want?"

"I'm assuming to concede."

"Already?"

"Yes, the writings on the wall."

"It's only nine thirty." Karen looked at her watch and sighed.

"You have a twenty-point lead. If the roles were reversed, I'd be advising you the same way. He can't recover from this."

Karen nodded, intertwined her fingers with Sarah's, and walked to a small desk in the back behind a set of file cabinets. Sarah sat on the edge of the desk as Karen took a deep breath.

"Hello, Walter?"

"Hello Representative, I just wanted to call and congratulate you and let you know I'll be supporting you in the November election."

"Thank you, Walter, I look forward to having you on the campaign trail."

"Enjoy the night. Good night, Representative."

"Good night, Walter."

"Call me Walt."

"Good night, Walt."

She hung up and looked at Sarah.

"I want to apologize right now for what's to come."

"Bad food, shaking hands and uncomfortable suits."

"Yes." Karen nodded. "You still want to marry me?"

"Hell yes, you know how power turns me on," Sarah teased and leaned her forehead on Karen's.

She'd won. Karen wondered if it would be enough for her mother's forgiveness.

* * * *

"Damn." Becca ogled Sarah's engagement ring as she held on to her hand with a grip reserved for lower primates like a gorilla, not a little sister. "Rich and successful."

"They do go hand in hand, but Karen's not rich."

"Please, this rock has to hurt your hand."

"The only thing hurting my hand is you, mongrel." Sarah pulled her hand free and shook it out. "Was Jens coming home for the party?"

"Mizzou is too far away for one weekend."

"I suppose." Sarah looked at the pictures of her family with Jens, Becca, and her.

She was nervous about this party and the fact in three days she was moving in with Karen. Their wedding had a floating date depending on election results. Still she wouldn't mind a year long engagement. Part of her fear came from the snide comments Karen made about a small wedding. Sarah had never wanted a huge wedding, but Karen had. Ashton told her. Right now, the rejection she felt from her mother ate away at her. Each day without a phone call or note, Sarah had noticed a decline in her. She wished she could make it better, but it had to be her mother's choice to come to the party later that day.

Sarah went to her childhood room and plopped on the bed. She spun her phone in her hand again.

"Hey lazy bones," her mother said as she came in the room and smacked Sarah's knee with a dishtowel. "This party may be for you, but you still need to help."

"I will in a minute." Sarah unconsciously spun the ring on her finger.

"What's up, Sarah?"

"Karen's mom. Did she RSVP?"

"Nope, you said she wouldn't or I would have called to check with her." Her mom picked at a loose string on her shirt. "I know you're nervous, but once she meets you I'm sure she'll see what her daughter does."

"Is that stock advice?"

"It's the lie your grandma told me about your dad's mom. Either way you two will be happy."

"I'll be down in a little bit," Sarah said as she scrolled through her contacts. "I just need to make a phone call."

"All right, I need help finding serving dishes."

With her mother out of the room, Sarah decided to make a phone call to Ash. Thirty minutes later, they were in a car on their way to the Schroeder's. Sarah tried to keep her calm as they wound around to the Schroeders' home on Lake Jane. Ashton pulled up the long driveway and Sarah saw a beautiful home with a wrap-around porch. By the front door, a swing rocked from the strong breeze and Sarah gripped Ashton's hand tightly. He was good for support she'd give him that.

"Now, her mother's bark is worse than her bite."

"Right."

Ashton knocked and Sarah slid behind him slightly.

"Ashton," the woman with an angular bob hair cut answered the door. Her eyes were a darker shade of caramel than Karen's, but the resemblance was unmistakable. "What brings...is that her?" Her face pursed as her body stiffened.

"I'm Sarah, Sarah Lindstrom." Sarah extended her hand, but then retracted when she was harshly rejected. "Before you passed judgment on me I just wanted to at least meet you."

"What you have done to my daughter—"

"I'm going to stop you right there, Beatrice, Bea, mama." Ashton flashed his killer smile and Karen's mom twitched. "We all know Kare Bear doesn't do anything she doesn't want to."

"Look, you can hate me for the rest of your life, but Karen's your daughter and she needs you. She won't admit it, but your approval means everything to her and it's killing me to see her so upset."

"Then you should've thought of that before you brainwashed her into being a...a...I can't even say it."

"Lesbian." Sarah straightened her back and stared into Mrs. Schroeder's eyes. "Whether you admit it or not, we both know Karen's been gay longer than our relationship, and you've known it somewhere deep inside. Again, you don't have to like me or even tolerate me, but if you cut Karen out of your life it will be a wound that will never heal."

Sarah turned on her heel and headed to Ashton's car. It had been a mistake. That woman would never accept any choice Karen made. At least now she knew it wasn't her that was the problem, but she would become the bandage to help Karen get through the loss.

164

* * * *

Karen rang the Lindstroms' doorbell and resettled the pasta salad she'd made in her hands. Okay, so she didn't make it, but she did scoop it out of the deli containers to the carrier dish.

"What are your intentions with my sister?" Sarah's little sister Becca growled as she yanked the door open.

"Um…I…what did I do?"

"Are you brainwashing her to become a Republican?" the girl with the blonde and black hair crossed her arms. "She's not you know. None of us are. We believe in abortion, sex changes, and a woman's right to carry a weapon."

"One of those are mine."

"You sure?"

"I…your name is Becca, right?" Karen asked.

"Is my sister playing protective crazy woman?" Sarah called from the kitchen as she walked to the front door.

"I had to," her sister confessed as she went from harsh to sweet. "Jens said it was my job."

"Of course he did." Sarah took the dish and kissed Karen on the cheek. "I apologize now for my family."

"I love it. Are any of my sisters coming?"

"Darlene and Helen are already here." Sarah led Karen to the backyard. Round, white tables were set up with plastic chairs around them. A long table had a variety of food on it with plates and drinks. Darlene's husband was helping Sarah's dad at the grill.

"I'm not going to help you anymore with debate prep if you pull that crap again," Helen said with a smile. "That was not the answer we'd discussed."

Helen hugged Karen and they each held on longer than they had in the past.

"No hogging her." Darlene bust in and got her own embrace. "I won't let her know you followed my advice on one question."

"I'm not sure it was all you." Karen pulled back and crinkled her nose at Darlene.

More guests poured in the backyard over the next hour, including the mafia members, some of Karen's staff including Howard, and some of Sarah's extended family. They all seemed genuinely happy to meet her. She and Sarah made the rounds at the tables in between small plates of food. Little kids were playing on an old swing set and Karen allowed herself to relax.

"Hello everyone," Patty yelled. "Can I have your attention?"

The talking quieted down to light murmurs.

"Thank you all for coming here today." Patty beamed and Sarah's dad, Sven, stood by her.

Sarah slid her arm around Karen's waist and leaned her head on Karen's shoulder.

"When Sarah came over about a month ago, I saw something had changed in her. It was pretty evident what had happened."

"She got some," Mandy yelled and Sarah covered her face with her hand.

"Amanda, don't mess with the vision of my sweet daughter."

"You don't live with her."

"Neither will you soon," Mary Beth said as she backhanded her.

"For those who've never met the Growing Strong Mafia…there they are. Did you know what you were getting into Karen?"

"I had been warned," Karen assured Patty.

"When you asked Sarah to marry you, you took on more than just the Lindstroms," Sven said. "You got that rowdy bunch, too."

"I see it as a bonus."

"That's because you haven't had to survive a sleepover." Sven shook his head.

"Can I get back to my speech?" Patty asked.

"I highly doubt it," Becca added.

"Fine." Patty grumbled. "Karen, you make my daughter happy and I'm so happy to invite you into my family."

"Thank…" Karen froze as she saw her father walk out the sliding glass door. A lump filled her throat and she squeezed Sarah tighter.

For a moment, the world stopped. Never had the sight of her father's high and tight haircut made her feel so happy. The weight on her shoulders dissipated…a moment later, the one on her chest completely disappeared as her mother came from behind him. Patty turned and brought her hands in prayer in front of her face. Karen looked at Dar and Helen, who both rushed to her.

"Did we interrupt?" her mother asked.

Karen's head swam and she wasn't sure if she should see her coming as a good thing or not. Part of her was still scared of rejection. Here it would hurt more because everyone had been so gracious.

"No," Patty said. "I was just finishing my speech welcoming your beautiful daughter into our family."

"They're not married yet," Beatrice bit, and then sucked in her lips. Karen's heart sank at the gesture as her head dipped. "But I have to say I am happy my daughter found someone who cares so much for her."

Karen's head shot up and she caught her mother's eyes.

"Although I'm not excited about her lifestyle choice and I may never agree with it, I do see why she finds comfort and love from Sarah."

"Does that mean she likes me?" Sarah whispered in Karen's ear.

"I'm really not sure," Karen replied under her breath.

"I look forward to getting to know Sarah better," Beatrice said. "And I hope Karen finds the happiness her sisters have."

Karen let go of Sarah and crossed to her mother. She was the first to hug, but eventually her mother softened and put her arms around Karen.

"I missed you, Mom."

"I missed you too, Kare Bear." Her mother placed a peck on her cheek. "You'll have to give me time, you know that, right?"

"Yes, Mom."

"I'm sorry I said you weren't my daughter." Beatrice wiped the tears from Karen's cheeks with her thumb. "I just wanted you to know that even I could make a mistake."

Epilogue

"Blessed is the influence of one true, loving human soul on another."
—George Eliot

November

"We'll keep the numbers scrolling on the bottom as we return to our regular news cast." The female reporter said as the story switched to one about a fire at an Apple Valley apartment building.

On the bottom, the Fourth District scrolled by about every eleven minutes. Sarah sat on the couch next to Karen as the Growing Strong Mafia girls hung out eating pizza and picking with each other.

"You know," Mandy said. "This is the most exciting election I've watched."

"In other words, it's the only election you watched," Gabbie said as she tossed a breadstick at Mandy.

"Details. No seriously, what is it—forty nine to fifty one?"

"On the last go round," Karen sighed, and Sarah could see the headache forming.

"I've got the lawyers ready if the margin doesn't get wider," Howard said.

"The lawyers." Karen leaned forward and rested her head on her hand. "Is that really necessary?"

"Old Barbie Blake has hers already writing up the recount petition." Howard's foot bounced, and Sarah swore he was drooling.

"Is he always like this?" She asked Karen.

"I've never had an election this close. And it is a national office."

Lawyers sat at the edge of the room with their laptops out. Sarah wondered how much they got paid to sit there at the ready.

"My mom wants a June wedding," Karen said. "She says the house is the best in June, but she is really confused on what we are to wear."

The hour grew later. Gabbie and Mary Beth said their good-byes. Tomorrow would be a hard day for Sarah at school staying up this late. She'd been spoiled during the primary. Now in a large ballroom a thousand supporters were waiting for Karen to come out and accept or concede the election. Hidden away in the waiting area they could avoid the loud noises and craziness...well, most of it.

"What the fuck?" Mandy spat, and Sarah woke up from where she'd been nodding off.

"What happened?" she asked, and Karen turned up the volume on the TV, but Mandy was looking at her phone.

"My mom's pregnant." Mandy held the phone up to Sarah so she could read the text and the two women shared a mutual revulsion. "I need to go tell Mary Beth."

"Yes, before she hears it from anyone else."

Now with only Karen and the guys in the room, Sarah stood up behind Karen and hugged her back.

"It's not getting wider yet," Karen said with a fierce face. "Why can't she just call and concede I won?"

"Would you?"

"I'm the bigger person. Of course I would."

"No you wouldn't." Sarah kissed Karen's neck.

"Probably not, but hey..." The screen cut to the ballroom where Barbara Blake was approaching the podium. "Shit, if she declares she won before me, I'm screwed."

"Why?"

"The first to declare is the first to win."

"What if she's conceding?"

"She would've called me first." Karen pulled away. "Howard, what the hell?"

"Shit," he said under his breath.

"*Hello all,*" Barbara said as she put her hands out to silence the crowd who were chanting Blake. "*Thank you all for your support. The numbers are too close to call tonight."* A supporter yelled. *"I love you, too. I've spoken to my legal team and we'll have to see where the numbers are in the morning. Right now Representative Schroeder has the upper hand, but in the light of a new day it might be something different. I will be here until the final vote is tallied."*

"She didn't do anything," Howard balked. "She didn't call herself the winner or loser."

"Now what?" Sarah asked.

"Now…we wait." Karen took Sarah's hand in hers and kissed her knuckles. "Are you with me?"

This wasn't a question for Sarah. She would support and love Karen until the end of their days. She'd found love that had been returned by the one person who could touch her in a way she didn't know she could be touched.

"Forever."

THE END

About the Author

Michel Prince is an author who graduated with a bachelor degree in History and Political Science. Michel writes young adult and adult paranormal romance as well as contemporary romance.

With characters yelling "It's my turn, damn it!!!" She tries to explain to them that alas, she can only type a hundred and twenty words a minute and they will have wait their turn. She knows eventually they find their way out of her head and to her fingertips and she looks forward to sharing them with you.

When Michel can suppress the voices in her head she can be found at a scouting event or cheering for her son in a variety of sports. She would like to thank her family for always being in her corner, and especially her husband for supporting her every dream and never letting her give up.

Michel has been awarded Elite Status with Rebel Ink Press in 2013, the service award for her local RWA chapter Midwest Fiction Writers in 2013 and 2014, won Sweetest Romance at IREA and is a PAN member of RWA. She lives in the Twin Cities with her husband, son, and dog, Bolt.

You may contact the author at:

www.michelprincebooks.com
www.facebook.com/michelprincebooks
https://twitter.com/michelprince1